# FitzDuncan

John J. Spearman

# DEDICATION

For Alicia, as always.

# OTHER BOOKS BY THIS AUTHOR

### *The Halberd Series*

*-Gallantry in Action*

*-In Harm's Way*

*-True Allegiance*

*-Surrender Demand*

### *The Pike Series*

*-Pike's Potential*

# ACKNOWLEDGMENTS

Dear Reader,
You are the purpose of this and all my books. Thank you for reading.
If you like what you have read, please leave a positive review on
Amazon.com or goodreads.com. If you did not like it, I'm sorry.

# 1

After unlocking the door to my rooms, I took the first step up the stairs in the dark. I caught a whiff of someone's putrid breath. I woke in a cell in the Palace of Justice. The light was dim. There was a torch outside on the wall but only a small barred window in the door to allow light in. My head hurt. Reaching up gingerly, there was a decent-sized lump above my right ear. I struggled to sit up and wished I hadn't. Moving upright made my head hurt and ears ring. Plus, it involved pushing up with my hand on the floor, which was covered with damp and a hint of slime. Who knows what mixture of bodily fluids was included in that cold ooze?

A few minutes later, one of the guards wandered by and peered through the bars in the door opening. I heard him grunt, then walk away. Some more time went by, quite a bit by my reckoning, and I heard footsteps again. The key was put in the lock and turned. The door opened with a creak, allowing more torchlight in. Sir Oliver West came in, holding a small stool. Swinging the stool down, he stepped over it and sat, looking at me with calm regard. Sir Oliver was the Principal of the City Watch, a service that combined the duties of a constabulary with fire protection.

"Why, Ollie?" I complained, rubbing the knot on my head.

"Caz, if I'd let you know I wanted to talk to you, would you have come?" he replied.

"Probably not," I admitted.

"Probably not," he snorted. "Probably would have left town like a hurricane, and only the good gods would know when you'd return."

"Still," I protested. "Your man gave me quite a knot. He's got a tooth rotten, too, I think, judging from the reek of his breath. And this is hardly the most hospitable quarters," I remarked, waving my hand, indicating the dim, dank cell. "These clothes are probably ruined. Come to think of it," I patted my side where I carried my money pouch, "where's my money?"

"Here," Ollie said, flipping it to me. I didn't catch it. It hit the floor with a satisfying thunk. "A bit over 200 ducats."

"Thank you, Ollie."

"Care to share with me why you're so flush?"

"I had a good night, at least until your goon bashed me in the head. I'm surprised he didn't take it."

"He did," Ollie replied with a shrug. "But I didn't let him keep it. And he does have a rotten tooth. It stinks."

"So, what did you want me for? You went to a fair amount of effort to make sure I didn't avoid you."

"What do you know of Miss Julienne Traval?" Ollie asked.

I gave him my most blank look. "Who?"

"Julienne Traval," he repeated, staring at me intently, looking for any reaction.

Fortunately, I had long ago learned not to betray much with my face. I started to shake my head slowly but stopped with a wince. Getting coshed made any movement of my head a bad idea. It worked out, though. All he saw was my grimace of pain.

"I don't believe I know her," I stated. "Is she attractive? Why do you ask?"

"She went missing this afternoon," Sir Oliver stated. "Actually, that's not fair to say. According to witnesses, she was nabbed this afternoon from Crown Street, just down from your place. A black hackney pulled up next to her, and two men jumped out, grabbed her, and threw her inside. She dropped her bag in the scuffle. They galloped away. Amongst the other items in her bag was a scrap of paper with your name and address."

"Huh," I grunted.

"Based on the direction she was heading, she would have just left from meeting you. Where were you this afternoon?"

"In a black hackney, waiting for Etienne Lavalle to come walking along, so I could kidnap her and hold her for ransom," I quipped cheekily, mistaking her name on purpose.

"Caz, don't," Sir Oliver warned.

"Don't, what?"

"Don't dig yourself any deeper into the hole you've started. The young lady met with you at half-past two. She stayed for almost an hour. You served her tea and gave her a handkerchief when she started to cry. When she left, she had regained her composure—her coloring was back to normal."

"If you know all that, why ask?" I retorted. My mind was awhirl—had Sir Oliver been watching me? Watching her? Did someone in the bookseller's shop talk?

"It's always a pleasure to watch you lie, Caz. You're so damned good at it," he admitted. "If I didn't know, I'd have believed you when you said you hadn't met her. I'm guessing she came to discuss her impending marriage. I presume she has misgivings about her fiancé."

I looked at him blankly. "Ollie," I said, "you know she came to meet me. That's bad enough. I won't discuss what help she sought from me. When she left, I had not decided whether I would take her problem on. I would have needed to discuss it with her father. Regardless, since she met with me in confidence, I'm afraid that conversation will have to remain between her and me."

"For someone who dances on both sides of the law," Sir Oliver noted, "and often on the wrong one, you sure can be a sanctimonious prig."

I shrugged in response.

"Miss Traval is engaged to marry Bergeron, the Viscount du Pais," Sir Oliver stated. "Her father, Herbert Traval, is an extremely wealthy merchant trader. He arranged the marriage because the Viscount is nearly penniless, having squandered his meager inheritance. The Viscount is, however, a close acquaintance of the Crown Prince. Mr. Traval is hoping that the marriage will benefit his business—that Bergeron will convince the Crown to steer business his way. As her dowry, Traval will gift the Viscount with a million ducats. Does that match with what she told you?"

I nodded, then winced again from the pain in my head.

"Good. I'm guessing she came to you because the Viscount has an extremely unsavory reputation. No woman in her right mind would want to marry such an animal. Unfortunately for her, Bergeron insisted on a marriage contract. If she tries to call off the marriage, he still gets the million. It's not hard to guess she is hoping that you can help her find a way to avoid marrying the pig and not cost her father the money. The only way that can happen is if Bergeron calls it off."

"As I said, I have not decided to take her problem on," I protested weakly. "I would need to discuss with her father what percentage of that million he would be willing to part with."

"I doubt he would be willing to pay your usual fee," Sir Oliver smirked.

I suppose I'd better tell you a bit about myself, so that this makes more sense. Hello. My name is Casimir FitzDuncan. I am the eldest son of Duncan Barry, Earl of the Eastern March. The Eastern March is the borderland on the east of the kingdom of Aquileia. The entire country is roughly 200 leagues east to west and 300 leagues from the coast in the south to the beginning of the perpetual snows, though human settlement is sparse further than 100 leagues from the southern coast.

As you may guess from my surname, I was born out of wedlock. I have two younger half-brothers who both stand to inherit once our father passes on. I doubt there will be any provision for me in his will—at least, that's what he's told me.

My mother was a maid who succumbed to my father's charm. When my father married, she was sent away. My grandfather gave her a small sum to set herself up as a seamstress in a town as far away from the March as possible. I've seen her since. She's a nice woman but hasn't played much of a role in my life since she left when I was three.

When my father married, grandfather insisted I stay in the household until Victoria, my father's wife, produced male heirs. That took longer than expected. Victoria tolerated my presence with icy civility. She certainly never displayed any sort of maternal affection. My father didn't have much time for me either, busy with the affairs of the March and away three weeks out of four. My grandfather raised me, and everything I am I owe to him.

Growing up, I had advantages. Tutors came and taught me reading, writing, and maths. My grandfather made sure I learned how to handle a sword. Some of the arms men taught me how to fight, which is not the same thing. The crucial difference is, when fighting for your life, there are no rules.

If I had any complaints, the only one I can remember is that playing with the children in the village was discouraged. I remember being lonely a lot as a boy. We lived in a fortified manor house. It wasn't quite a castle in terms of size and grandeur, but it had all the same defensive features. With thick stone walls, it was cold inside for nine months of the year, pleasant for two and unbearably hot the last month of the summer.

When I was thirteen, Victoria gave birth to my first half-brother, Edwin, and fifteen when she issued forth Percival. When Edwin was born, they sent me away to school. They did not want me in the house after that—my presence was no longer bearable. Even my grandfather agreed I should leave. My grandfather was the only member of the family who showed me any affection. He stayed in contact after I was sent away. He and I exchanged letters regularly. After leaving home for school, I was permitted to come back only once. The one time I was allowed to return home was for my grandfather's funeral. I was not permitted to stay in the family home. I paid for a room at the inn, down in the town. My grandfather's last letter to me commented on the weak chins of his legitimately born grandsons and his gut feeling that neither would amount to much. At the funeral, I saw the evidence, not that it matters.

School was the first extended exposure I had to others my age. So it was for many of us, except for those who came from large families. We hadn't learned how to get along with others, and nearly everyone had his insecurities. For protection, more emotional than physical—at least at first—groups formed. The sons of the landed nobility considered themselves superior and formed associations based on the ties their parents had with other families. Boys whose parents were wealthy merchants banded together to protect and support one another since they were usually the targets of the scions of the aristocracy. Then there was me.

From the moment anyone heard my name, I was put into my own category—bastard. According to the customs of Aquileia, my surname, FitzDuncan, means illegitimate son of Duncan. There was no one else at school named Fitz-anything. That meant there was no group that would accept me and all groups felt free to belittle and sometimes attack me. The lessons the arms men had taught me were occasionally useful. During school breaks, I stayed on campus. Thirteen- and fourteen-year-old boys don't have the strength of character to defy the judgment of the group. Since I had grown up largely alone, I was accustomed to it. Later, on three occasions, friends whose families were unconcerned about my illegitimate status invited me to stay with them. At 16 and 17, there were some boys willing to measure me on my own merits instead of my surname.

After I graduated from school, my grandfather had arranged a place in the army, with the Rangers. I spent seven years with the Rangers. We guarded the mountain passes on the western border of the realm. Because I was the son of an earl and had been to school, they made me an officer. My troopers did not care about my last name. Growing up, I had seen how my father and grandfather treated the men under their command. Their good examples gave me an advantage in the Rangers. My fellow officers still snubbed me, but my men liked me and had confidence in me. They didn't care about my social standing. Neither did the Rhetians.

The area of the kingdom where we served is called the Western March. Our neighbors, the Rhetian Empire, had long coveted our land. It had been generations since they had tried a full-scale invasion, but raids back and forth across the border were a regular occurrence for both sides.

The Rhetians worshipped their own god. They only had one. We have twelve. That was one reason the Rhetians hated us. The three Major Gods are the gods of the sky, the ocean and the land. There are also nine Minor Gods: a male god of love (who was also the god of fertility), a female goddess of love (her area was romance and sexual pleasure), a goddess of good fortune, a goddess of health, a goddess of wisdom, a god of crafts and smithing, a god of travel and commerce, a goddess of art and literature and a goddess of war. Besides those, there is also the Lord of the Seven Hells, who is the god of the underworld and afterlife. Our religion says he was originally one of the Major Gods, but the other three cast him down because of his dark soul.

The Western March differs from the Eastern March where I grew up. The border in the west was marked by a mountain range. The eastern border was a narrow, shallow river that cut through grasslands. The grassy plains stretched as far as the eye could see. Small groups of horse nomads would ride out of the grasslands to raid our villages often. Every few years, the nomads would attack in large groups. My grandfather claimed they did not raid for plunder (though they took whatever they could). He believed the raids were a rite of passage for the tribes. I have no idea what gods they worship.

It was during my third year in the Rangers that grandfather died. He made a small provision for me in his will. Being Earl of the Eastern March carries a serious military commitment but not much in the way of money. The Earl of the Western March, on the other hand, is supported by the Rangers, funded by the Crown. The Earl of the Eastern March receives no assistance. It's difficult to amass much of a fortune when most of your income goes to support your military readiness. Still, in grandfather's will, I was given an annual allowance of one hundred ducats. It was enough to survive upon if I were willing to lead a humble existence.

He also left me a sword, which I still carry. It is a finer blade than any I have seen, before or since. A rapier with a blade of nine parts and a swept hilt, it is a masterpiece of the swordsmith's art. The blade is, of course, a single piece. The nine parts refer to the different composition of the steel with which each section is made. It is stiff at the hilt and gradually more flexible at the tip. Looking at it, you can't tell where one section ends and the next begins—they are melded together with tremendous skill.

While a member of the Rangers, I spent time with the Crown Prince, Albert, whom I did not like, and his younger brother, Wim. I might have been friends with Wim if my circumstances were different, but my being a bastard made that impossible. Our relations were cordial and to this day, he always had a friendly word for me whenever our paths crossed in polite company. Unlike his brother, he was approachable, friendly, a good soldier and a good comrade.

After seven years in the Rangers, I reached the rank of Captain. It would take at least another seven years to climb the next rung on the ladder unless I had money or an influential relative to back me. I had neither, so I decided to leave. Upon leaving the Rangers, I went to the capital, also named Aquileia. I had no idea what sort of career I would follow. My grandfather's allowance would not enable me to stay in the city for long—I needed another source of income. I took a set of rooms above a bookseller and set about trying to determine what I wanted to be and what course I should pursue.

From school and my exposure there to the sons of the nobility and the wealthy merchant class, I had acquired a taste for the finer things. That appetite was honed by seven years of living rough with the Rangers. I bounced around Aquileia for a couple of months, my discharge pay evaporating at an alarming rate, with no better idea of what to do than when I arrived. Fortune smiled upon me, though, in the form of a friend from school who came to me with a problem.

He found me on the street as I was returning to my rooms. He invited himself up, saying he needed my help. Freddy had been one of the better sort at school. Some of my schoolmates would not deign to speak to me, given my illegitimate birth. Once we were older, it never seemed to bother Freddy, though he was as noble-born as any. He was one of the three schoolmates who invited me to his home.

He followed me up the stairs to my rooms and, once we sat, he explained his problem. Freddy had lost a ring in a card game by offering it as surety for a bet. He did not have the money on his person to cover the bet and felt certain he had the winning hand. The winner suggested the ring would be proof that Freddy would come back with the money, with a bland assurance that Freddy would get it back when he delivered. The ring was a family heirloom. Freddy suspected that the game had been rigged and he had been cheated, but he had no proof other than a hunch. He showed up with the money the next day for the amount of the wager (10,000 ducats!), but its new owner refused to give it back. He demanded ten times that. Freddy needed to regain the ring before his father learned he had lost it but had nowhere near the money to pay what the new owner demanded.

From our school days, Freddy remembered I was good at cards. It was one of the few forms of entertainment we were allowed. I rarely lost, and usually only when I meant to (there were times, given my uncertain perch in society, when it would be counterproductive to win). Freddy wanted me to win his ring back and expose its new owner as a cheat. He offered to bankroll my card play initially. I would keep any winnings and he would give me, in addition, half the amount of the lost wager—5,000 ducats—when I recovered the ring.

It was an unusual request, but it captured my interest. I knew and did not like his tormentor, Sir Edmund Tourville, which made it even more attractive. It took a few weeks. Without belaboring you with the details, I succeeded. At the end of this adventure, I found myself in possession of nearly 7,500 ducats, from my reward and my winnings. It was not enough to support myself indefinitely, given my expensive wants, but it did provide me with a few years' time before I needed to establish a career.

A few months later, an acquaintance of Freddy's approached me with his own problem. Some letters he had written to a lady friend (who was not his wife) had fallen into unscrupulous hands and he was being blackmailed. Freddy had shared my name with him and suggested he contact me. The blackmailer had demanded 5,000 ducats for the letters. I obtained the letters and received 2,500 ducats in compensation from the writer.

That set me on my current path. I invested a good portion of my money in buying the bookseller from whom I was renting rooms. My ownership was to remain a secret. If anyone inquired, I was merely a lodger. I insisted that the staff of the shop maintain an absolute blind eye as far as my comings and goings, and any visitors that might call looking for me. Up to now, that level of discretion had been maintained. The shop more than paid for itself, generating a small additional income.

Word of mouth spread, quietly and discreetly, from my first two 'clients.' I was someone who could help in difficult situations when no other solution seemed possible. I established a pattern. My fee would be half the value of whatever needed to be recovered. Now, seven years along, I'd helped a dozen people recover something of value discreetly, in circumstances where other, legal, means of recovery were unavailable. During this time, Sir Oliver and I had crossed paths, and swords, on a number of occasions. I respected him. He struck me as an honest man and not someone I would classify as an enemy. He was bound by the strictures of the law. I was not.

My public persona was that of a man-about-town, living off an inheritance from my grandfather. That, as I explained, was a false facade. My grandfather's bequest was nowhere near what I needed to maintain myself in the style I enjoyed. I lived comfortably but not lavishly. I was occasionally, but not always, seen on the fringes of 'better' society. I was a son of the Earl of the Eastern March and, even though I was illegitimate, that thin association with nobility kept some doors open for me—but only partly. For instance, I was not allowed to become a member of the club where I had won nearly 200 ducats the night before, but I was allowed to enter as someone's guest.

Miss Traval had indeed inquired about gaining my help in freeing her from the impending doom of her marriage. Her father was not sympathetic—seeming to care more about the business opportunities the marriage might bring than any harm that might befall his daughter. That had been the stumbling block for me. I had not agreed to help her since I suspected her father would not welcome, and certainly would not reward, my interference.

I responded to Sir Oliver's comment about my usual fee. "I suspect not," I replied. "In fact, I doubt whether he would support my involvement at all. As I said, I had not made up my mind whether to help her. I was leaning towards turning her down, though I certainly understand her reluctance to marry Bergeron."

"She is quite attractive," Sir Oliver commented. "I thought that might sway you."

"That is perhaps why I did not refuse to help immediately," I answered. "Now, I need a favor from you, Ollie. Please tell me how you knew about my meeting with her. I don't want to have to sack the entire staff at the shop."

He sighed. "No one in your shop, Caz."

"Then where was your watcher?"

"Across the way. You didn't close the curtains."

"How did your watcher know to be there?" I asked.

"A certain someone overheard Miss Traval talking with a certain someone else about her predicament. Your name was overheard. It reached her father. He contacted Bergeron, the Viscount contacted the Crown Prince, and it rolled downhill to me."

"That helps explain all this," I admitted, "since knocking me out and dragging me down here is a bit heavy-handed, especially for you."

"Seven hells, Caz," Sir Oliver said. "I know you had nothing to do with the abduction. She arrived at your place unannounced and was taken immediately after. I know you can work quickly, but there's no way you arranged her kidnapping without leaving the room. You're here for appearances."

"Rounding up likely suspects, eh? Are you apologizing, and by some chance, I missed it?"

West rolled his eyes. "Fine. Sorry for dragging you here like this, even though you would have run away if I'd tried to contact you by any other method."

"Apology accepted. Why are we still down here in this shithole?"

"Fair enough," he said, standing and offering me a hand up.

We left the cell and climbed the stairs to the ground floor. I was still a bit wobbly, and my head was pounding. When we reached the top, the light was better and I could see the smears and smudges on my clothes from spending the night in the cell. They looked awful and smelled worse. We climbed another flight of stairs and reached his office. I sat gingerly on the edge of a chair, not wanting to smear the upholstery with whatever was on my clothes.

"My blade?" I asked him.

"Left on the stairs to your rooms."

"Your watcher saw the abduction?" I asked.

"Yes."

"Did her family later report her missing, or did the City Watch tell them?"

"We informed them of what was seen."

"What was their response?"

"Rage. Indignation. Demands that she be found. The usual," Sir Oliver answered.

"The contract Traval signed with du Pais—how enforceable is it?" I asked.

"I understand the contract is quite clear. The Viscount gets the million if the marriage is called off for any reason."

"What if she dies?"

"Any reason," Sir Oliver repeated.

"Then the father probably didn't take her, or he would have admitted it. He needs the marriage to go through, or else he pays the million and gets nothing in return. Without a bride, du Pais has no reason to influence anyone on Traval's behalf."

"That's probably true," Sir Oliver agreed.

"So, who do you think took her?" I asked.

Sir Oliver scrutinized me, wrinkling his nose, before answering.

"Bergeron—to keep her from running away, though he has already denied taking her. Perhaps there is another suitor, or her friends did it to help her escape marrying the Viscount. The strongest possibility is a third party who knows of the marriage contract and will demand ransom from Traval."

I thought a bit about Sir Oliver's situation. "Have *you* questioned du Pais?"

He shook his head.

"Do you think there's another suitor, or her friends were involved?"

"I can certainly understand the girl wanting to run away from a marriage like this," he said. "But I doubt it."

"That points us in the direction of a true kidnapper, though du Pais cannot be entirely trusted."

Sir Oliver nodded.

"So, why are you telling me this?"

"I want you to dig into it."

"What's in it for me?"

"You get to rescue a damsel in distress. The satisfaction of doing a good deed — "

"No financial compensation, in other words," I interrupted.

To his credit, he didn't laugh. He gave me a pained look. I nodded in understanding.

"You can't even pay my expenses, can you?" I asked.

He shook his head. "Only minor ones, I'm afraid."

"I can't believe you're asking me this after bashing me in the head and throwing me in that slime-encrusted hole."

He did not respond for a few beats. "I believe I told you it was for appearances. When a request comes from the castle, I need to give it the appearance of diligence since I already knew I could not provide any meaningful information as a result of speaking with you. If I hadn't done it, they would have found someone who would. Their interrogation would be much more vigorous and unpleasant. Plus, I would be on shaky ground."

"Why do you want *me* to unravel this?" I asked.

"I don't know the young lady," he admitted, "so I can't say I have a personal motive. The practice of rich commoners marrying impoverished nobles has been going on for hundreds of years, and it never bothered me in the slightest. Perhaps it's her father and Bergeron. They are both so repugnant. It offends my sense of justice. I can't do anything about it. You can. I think someone took her for ransom. I think you can find her."

"Yet it doesn't offend you to put on a show that involves injuring me and ruining a set of my clothes? Why in the world would I take this on? There's nothing in it for me except possibly making an enemy of the Viscount and this Traval. If I don't find her, I get the blame. Traval has enough bully boys in his employ that I'll likely end up floating face down in the river in a day or two. It would be no more to him than swatting away an annoying bug. If I try to question du Pais further, I offend him and his friend at the castle."

"Of course, her situation bothers me," I continued. "How could it not? But unlike you, <u>Sir</u> Oliver, I'm not a baronet. I don't have a government job or a small estate to which I can retire. I can't afford to be offended, even though I may feel the same outrage as you."

"I'm asking you because I respect you," he said simply. "You have a certain autonomy I lack. I believe it will be necessary to work outside the law to find her. It's ironic—achieving justice will require breaking the law. I've watched you for the last few years since our paths first crossed. You have always worked to achieve justice, even though you don't always follow the law. I can't think of anyone who would be able to accomplish this other than you."

That statement, and the pained look on his face that accompanied it, silenced me. I stared at the edge of his desk. I hadn't imagined that the respect I grudgingly gave him would be returned.

"Ollie, if I do this, you're going to owe me," I said quietly. "I may never need to collect, but you'll owe me. As a man of honor, you won't be able to refuse, even if it tarnishes your reputation. I will not abuse it and will make every attempt to maintain discretion, but if a circumstance arises where I need to redeem this favor, it may put you in an awkward position. Are you comfortable with that?"

He nodded gravely. He had already considered that. I didn't know whether to believe him. That thought saddened me.

I left the Palace of Justice shortly after and returned to the bookseller. The former owner, Lyle Forteney, still ran the place. Everyone assumed he still owned it. I didn't interfere as long as the establishment continued to be profitable. We met once a month to go over accounts. Both of us liked the arrangement. Plus, I had a well-stocked library to enjoy. It was rare that I ever asked him to get the employees to do anything outside of their normal duties in the shop. Today, I needed help. I asked Lyle to have a couple of the employees draw and heat some water for a bath.

In front of the employees, he treated my request as though I were still renting the rooms above the shop. He badgered me about adding it to my rent. Ordinarily, we would engage in a bit of good-natured back-and-forth, but today, my head hurt, my clothes stank, and I was in no mood for haggling. I merely nodded and trudged upstairs. I found my blade on the landing.

He followed me after a bit. "What the hell happened to you?" he asked.

"Someone brained me when I came in last night. I had an unpleasant morning and now I'm trying to regroup."

"Your clothes are a mess. Smell bad too. Should I send someone for Placida?"

Placida was the woman who cleaned my rooms and did my laundry once a week. "If I have any hope of salvaging these," I said, pointing to my clothing, "probably a good idea to get her now. She's not due for a couple of days otherwise."

"Is everything okay, Caz?" he inquired.

"It should be," I said, with a confidence I didn't quite feel.

Lyle left. A few minutes later, they started bringing hot water up for my bath. While I waited, I unloaded most of the contents of my money pouch into my strongbox. I kept about 20 ducats, most of it in smaller coins. It still gave the pouch a satisfying heft.

When the bath was ready, I stripped off my stained and pungent clothes and eased my way into the hot water. Immediately, the heat began to soothe the aches from spending the night unconscious on the cold stone floor of the cell. I washed thoroughly, trying to rid my body of the memory of the slime-encrusted floor. I hadn't gotten that dirty—it was more how it had made me feel. None of this helped the ache in my head, though.

# 2

After scrubbing, I lay there until the water cooled, pondering the problem of Miss Traval. Her father could hardly have chosen a worse person as a husband for his daughter. I knew Bergeron by reputation, and his reputation was dark and disturbing. I could understand why he would insist on a marriage contract of this type.

The Viscount du Pais was the scion of one of the oldest aristocratic families in the kingdom. They had managed to retain their standing through two previous civil wars—by changing sides at the most opportune times. The du Pais family resented all the 'new' nobility created when the members of the winning side in each conflict were rewarded.

The Barry family (of which I was an illegitimate offshoot) were named lords of the Eastern March after the last civil war, generations earlier. My many times great grandfather, Douglas, had been a supporter of Robert Gau when he won the throne by defeating his distant cousin. Gau became King Robert and Douglas Barry, then merely a minor baronet, was elevated to guard the Eastern March.

Many of these newer noble families had eclipsed the du Pais clan since then in terms of wealth, power and prestige. The du Pais, of course, resented this. They stayed fixed within a circle composed of a small group of similar old families. They intermarried among themselves, rather than allying with what they considered to be a 'jumped-up' or more recently ennobled clan. This practice ensured the old nobility's decline—without new blood and, more importantly, fresh resources, the older noble families were doomed to a slow death. For this reason, Bergeron's betrothal to a commoner was extremely unusual.

The du Pais clan had also long been rumored to practice the dark arts. There were still many in the kingdom, mostly the lower-classes, who believed in magic. Every little town or hamlet had a hedge witch who sold potions for love, health, fertility, indigestion and the like. Most hedge witches claimed to be disciples of the Minor Gods and Goddesses. The magic attributed to the du Pais clan was not of this sort. The dark arts were focused on poisons and curses. According to legend, torture of innocent victims, ritual dismemberment, human sacrifice, rape of virgins and other despicable crimes were said to increase one's power, granted to them by the Lord of the Seven Hells.

As the only son, Bergeron inherited everything that was left when his parents disappeared under mysterious circumstances six years earlier. Their bodies were later found on the bank of the Yoder River. Though badly rotted, there was still evidence that the couple had been mutilated before suffering a gruesome death. The general belief was that he had killed them, but there was no proof.

For all their supposed expertise in the dark arts, it certainly had not helped the du Pais clan prosper. The new Viscount inherited the estate and the ancestral home, located less than ten leagues to the north of the city. The manor was apparently in need of substantial repair, with only one-third of the building livable. In cash, there was less than 100,000 ducats. Income from tenant farmers was less than 5,000 ducats annually.

Bergeron had expensive taste and expensive friends, not the least of which was Albert, the Crown Prince. He and Albert had gone to school together and had become close. Bergeron was one of the small circle around Albert. Their preferred forms of misbehavior included things like rape, random beatings of people they encountered late at night after they'd been drinking, cheating at cards and fixing horse races.

When I served in the Rangers with Albert, during the nearly three years we were in the same unit, he never talked to me. He was my commanding officer for a time yet never spoke to me, even when I was standing right in front of him. Instead, he would turn to his aide and say, "Tell FitzDuncan this," or "Have FitzDuncan do that." It was juvenile and contemptuous. It never failed to irritate me, though I tried mightily not to show it.

Bergeron was the same sort. The last time I'd encountered him was at the Queen's Cup—the premier steeplechase race in the kingdom—a couple of years earlier. Someone, I think it was Freddy, tried to introduce us. Bergeron acted as though he hadn't heard. I pulled Freddy away gently before he reacted and told him we'd already met.

Freddy had complained quietly to me, "That's just rude. He pretended not to hear me."

"It's not you, Freddy. It's me," I explained. "He and his friends don't acknowledge my existence."

"That's still going on? I thought everyone would have outgrown that," Freddy commented.

Freddy then, in compensation for the snub perhaps, filled me in on all the gossip surrounding Bergeron. He told me that the Viscount was spending his inheritance rapidly. Being friends with the Crown Prince came at a cost—the Crown Prince expected a free ride wherever he went.

The water in the tub was now unpleasantly cool, and I stood up. I felt better, except for the ache in my noggin. I also had an idea about how I could begin to unravel what had happened to Miss Traval. Freddy seemed to be a logical place to start. Before I could begin pursuing that angle, I needed to dress or Placida would catch me naked. As it was, I had just fastened my belt when she knocked. I showed her my soiled clothes. She wrinkled her nose, saying, "Oh, Mr. Fitz... I don't know if I can save them."

"Do your best," I asked. "It's not your fault, so if you can't, I won't be angry with you."

"What did you roll around in?" she asked.

"The Palace of Justice," I answered with a smile. "Sir Oliver West wanted to talk to me. He didn't think I'd respond to a more polite invitation."

"He's probably right," she commented in a tone of disapproval. Placida had no idea what I did, but she knew it was something that was disreputable and likely criminal. She liked the money I paid her, though.

After I bundled her out, I sat and thought some more. Who would benefit from Miss Traval's disappearance? The Viscount, certainly. His marriage contract paid off regardless. Her father, probably not. Without his daughter linking him to du Pais, the Viscount had no obligation to influence anyone on Traval's behalf. The father's only reason to kidnap his daughter would be to prevent her from running away. There was always a possibility that Miss Traval had another suitor, but I doubted any young man would dare to make an enemy of her father. Still, I would need to look into it. I would need to learn who her friends are and which of them would be the one to know such a secret. The most likely proposition was that someone had taken her and would demand a ransom. That demand had not yet been made.

Until the kidnapper surfaced asking for ransom money, the only loose thread I could grasp was the Viscount. It would be easier to start there. With him eliminated as a suspect, then I could start beating the bushes to try to find her kidnapper.

I finished dressing, which meant donning a collar and cravat, a waistcoat and clean boots. I buckled my blade on and added a jacket, and set off to find Freddy. His house was about twenty minutes away by foot.

Earlier, on the way back from Palace of Justice, I hadn't noticed but now could tell it must have rained overnight. The normal odor of the streets was reduced. The air was now cool and dry—less humid than the day before. I rang the bell. Freddy's manservant answered. He looked down his nose at me.

"Is Lord Rawlinsford in?" I asked politely.

"I'll see."

The servant did not move.

"Is that Caz?" came a voice from the interior. "If it is, let him in, man."

The servant continued looking down his nose. "It appears Lord Rawlinsford is receiving."

He turned sideways but did not move out of my way.

"Caz?" Freddy called again.

"Your man won't let me in, Freddy," I responded.

"Damnit, Theo!" Freddy barked. "Let him in."

"As you wish, milord," the servant responded.

He moved only a half-step backward. I could, if I twisted myself carefully, just make it past him without touching him. Tempted though I was to lower my shoulder and drive it into his stomach, I squeezed by. Theo closed the door behind me with a slam. He certainly did not offer to take my jacket.

I was pulling it off as I proceeded in. Freddy saw me pulling my arm free. He shook his head, his nostrils flaring.

"Theo! Come get my guest's jacket and hang it up," he ordered.

Theo stalked into the room. He held out his hand as though my jacket were something repellent. He took it with the very tips of his finger and thumb, holding it as far away from himself as possible.

As he left the room, Freddy asked, "Shut the door on your way out, Theo."

Theo slammed it almost as hard as he had shut the front door.

"I get the distinct impression your man does not like me," I commented.

"My man!?!" Freddy snorted. "If he were my man, I'd sack him on the spot. He's my father's. He thinks he's here to keep an eye on me and report back to dad. He believes it's his duty to keep me away from vile company and immoral behavior."

"I was going to say," I commented. "I don't recall your previous man being this unpleasant."

"That was Roger. He's back with the family now. Dad sent Theo to me because he couldn't tolerate having Theo around anymore. Dad thinks it's hilarious. Theo writes him a report every week about who I've seen and what I've done, all in the most disapproving tone. Last time I was home, Dad shared his reports with me, laughing until his sides hurt. I suspect that when it's time for us to go, you'll see he hasn't hung your jacket. You'll find it dropped on the floor. Anyway, enough about Theo. Have a seat. Can I offer you a drop of sherry?"

"After the time I've had, a drop of sherry sounds quite welcome. Thank you."

"What brings you by?" he asked while pouring us each a glass.

"Actually, I need your help, Freddy."

"You? Need my help? That's a twist," he said, handing me my glass.

"Freddy, before I get into the details, I must ask for your complete discretion. It certainly would not be good to have Theo including any of it in his reports."

"Then drink up and we'll go for a stroll," Freddy suggested, miming someone holding his ear up to a wall.

"Perhaps we should visit a house of ill-repute, just to help Theo make his next report spicier."

Freddy laughed, then drained his glass. I followed his example. We rose, left the room, and headed to the entrance. As Freddy predicted, my jacket was in a heap on the floor. I picked it up, dusted it off, and put it on.

As we left, Freddy called out, "We're leaving, Theo. We're planning on gambling, drinking to excess and sharing the company of women with loose morals. Don't stay up."

A few steps out the door, and my stomach rumbled quite loudly. Apparently, the taste of sherry had reminded it I hadn't eaten since the night before. As it was now past mid-afternoon, it decided to make its desires known.

Freddy smiled. "I was going to ask, 'where to?' but I think you just answered that. Feeling a bit peckish?"

"I've had an unusual day," I explained, "and haven't fit a meal into the program yet. If you don't mind?"

"Certainly not," he replied. "It's a bit early, but that just means we can begin the drinking to excess earlier. Now, as for my discretion, you know you can count on it, Caz. What on earth could I help you with?"

I began to explain the events of the last 26 hours. I paused while we entered an inn that we knew served decent food, the Foaming Boar. I knew the owner from serving in the Rangers. He had retired as a Sergeant after 25 years of service. He took his retirement payout and bought the inn. Carl Stensland was doing good business. After we'd been served and the innkeeper left us alone, I resumed. Freddy paid close attention.

"So," I said, putting my hands flat on the table, "when you and I last ran into du Pais, you mentioned he was burning through his inheritance."

"Oh, it's long gone now," Freddy commented. "He's gone into debt— quite a bit of debt. From what I've heard, the income from tenant rents won't even cover half of his interest costs. He borrowed money from two different sources, neglecting to tell either about the other. Each one thought his interest would be paid from the rents, which is why they extended him funds in the amount they did. His creditors just learned of the other's existence. Du Pais failed to meet his obligations to them on time. When both of them sent messengers to visit du Pais and 'remind' him of his tardiness, their representatives met on his doorstep."

"How long ago did this happen?" I asked.

"Late last week—about five or six days ago," Freddy confirmed.

"Is du Pais still a part of Albert's inner circle?" I asked.

"Albert has the title, so he's technically the leader of that band of degenerates, but du Pais is really in charge. He feeds Albert's ego and Albert does what du Pais suggests, except for one thing."

"What's that?" I asked.

"Albert still expects everyone else to pay for everything. I don't think he is quite aware of how expensive it is to be his friend. Even if he did know, I doubt he would care. He certainly wouldn't offer to help the Viscount. I would imagine du Pais has kept his financial situation a secret from Albert. Albert would drop him like a hot rock if he knew du Pais was broke."

"This does not bode well for Miss Traval," I surmised.

Freddy shook his head. "I fear not. If du Pais gets the money regardless of whether he marries her, and he needs that money immediately, I would be looking for her body if he took her. Except — "

"Except what?" I asked.

"The du Pais clan is one of the old ones," Freddy said. "And they believe in the dark arts. I think it's a bunch of bunkum myself. Still, du Pais had a reputation for being able to perform tricks."

"Tricks? What kind of tricks?"

Freddy shook his head dismissively. "The same kind you see from mountebanks on the street. Making flames come out his fingers, coins disappearing and reappearing, that kind of thing. Enough to convince someone weak-minded that he did possess some actual skill. Albert and his cronies are convinced."

"So, what does this have to do with things?" I asked, trying to get Freddy back on topic.

"Right. Because du Pais probably fancies himself a practitioner of the dark arts, or has convinced his friends that he is, he might want to make use of Miss Traval in some way. We should go talk to my cousin Lucy."

"I haven't met her," I admitted.

"Her grandmother was my great-aunt Nancy. Nancy came from one of *those* families, like the du Pais. She was a believer in all that nonsense—crazy as a trapped badger, but they're all a bit in-bred these days. She hated all of us, especially her husband. It's astounding they ever had a child, but they did, Lucy's mother. The older Nancy grew, the more unpleasant, until Lucy was born. She claimed Lucy was a kindred spirit. She latched onto Lucy and tried to teach her all that nonsense."

"Does Lucy believe in all that?" I asked.

"Well," Freddy began, "she doesn't *dis*believe if that makes sense. Lucy believes in a lot of things."

"Again, what does this have to do with Miss Traval?"

"Right. Again, Lucy would know more, but I think that despoiling a virgin on a special day is supposed to bind you to the Lord of the Seven Hells and grant you dramatically increased power. I'm sure the ritual is more

18

complicated and involved than that."

"Let's go find Lucy."

We settled our bill with the innkeeper and departed. Freddy led the way. As we walked, he told me more about Lucy.

"The rest of the family has nearly disowned her because she's engaged in trade. They like to pretend she doesn't exist. Plus, she's different."

"Trade?" I inquired.

"That's part of it. She has a shop," Freddy answered. "She's an herbalist."

"She sells herbs?"

"Well..." Freddy drew this out, "... yes, but... If she were in a country village, they'd consider her a hedge witch. Here, in the city, people pretend not to believe in such things, so she's an herbalist. She does good business, though, so there must be something to it. As I said, Lucy believes in a lot of different things. The family thinks it's scandalous."

"That's she might be some sort of witch?"

Freddy shook his head quickly. "That doesn't bother them at all. We tolerate a great deal of eccentricity. No, their disapproval comes from her having a shop. The family believes the only acceptable way to make a living is with income generated from our land, or as a professional."

"Professional?"

"Doctor, lawyer or priest," Freddy explained. "Being a merchant is unacceptable."

"But, if Lucy does have some kind of magical ability, even slightly, then she is a sort of professional," I countered.

"Exactly!" Freddy exclaimed. "I've tried to make that same analogy, but it's fallen on deaf ears. The family is willing to tolerate a relative who claims to be a witch, but none of them actually believe she is."

I looked at Freddy quizzically. "What do you believe?"

"There are times when I'm convinced she is, but then I talk myself out of it."

We reached the square Freddy had mentioned. Her shop was directly in front of us. We entered. Opening the door caused a bell to jingle. It made a light, cheery sound. There were two customers, both women, looking at some items. Another woman with an unruly mop of long blonde hair had her back to us and was retrieving a jar from a shelf. Without turning around, she called out, "Hi Freddy. I'll be with you in a tic."

She turned around, giving us a smile, and took the jar to the two women. She was pretty, but I sensed she didn't think so. Her dress was loose and flowing, unlike the current fashion. Freckles adorned her face. Looking at her, I felt her happiness and contentment, and also a hint of curiosity about me. I noticed, even at a distance, that her eyes were the palest blue I'd ever seen. I was already slightly perplexed that she had known it was Freddy without turning around but reasoned she might have seen us through the front window as we approached.

After she finished with her customers, she came to us. She approached Freddy and gave him a kiss on the cheek. She turned to me.

"You're his friend, the bastard," she said after she clasped my hands.

"Excuse me?" I protested.

She looked slightly disappointed. "I forgot to tell you, Caz. Lucy is quite direct. It puts some people off."

"Right. So, you've told her all about me, then?"

Freddy blushed slightly, shaking his head.

She was still holding my hands lightly. I looked at her. She smiled shyly. My confusion grew. It must have shown on my face. She let go of my hands.

"You're his friend," she explained, "and one he values, or he wouldn't have brought you by."

I shrugged in agreement. "But — "

"You were born out of wedlock," she stated. "It shows in your aura."

"My what?"

"Your aura. Everybody has one," she stated in a matter-of-fact tone. "Yours clearly shows you were born out of wedlock."

I raised my eyebrows in response.

"You're not a believer," she sighed. "You have a headache, too. I can help you with that."

"I do have a headache," I admitted, more curious now. "And I am a bastard," I replied. "Casimir FitzDuncan, milady," I said with a small bow.

She smiled brightly, and her eyes twinkled. "There's hope for you yet, Casimir FitzDuncan. You're the one Freddy brought home from school years ago. I remember hearing about it. So, Freddy, what brings you to my thoroughly disreputable shop?"

"Caz and I have a number of questions about the dark arts."

She wrinkled her face in distaste. "Let me close the shop," she said. "It wouldn't do to have anyone interrupt us. I can give Caz something for his head, too."

She went to the door and locked it, pulling the shade down. She lowered the shades on the shop windows. Returning to us, she opened a drawer and pulled out a small bag. From the bag, she retrieved a piece of thin bark.

"Chew on this, slowly and thoroughly," she said. "It will taste bitter. Grind it up until it's all gone. I'll give you some tea in a bit to get rid of the taste."

She led us up a flight of stairs to her rooms. There was a parlor and she gestured for us to sit. I took a seat in an armchair. I sensed a presence over my left shoulder. I leaned forward and twisted around to look. A barn owl was perched just behind me. He looked down at me for a moment, then pulled his head up and closed his eyes. Lucy went into her kitchen and busied herself, presumably making tea.

When she returned, she cocked her head. "Interesting," she said.

"What's interesting?" Freddy asked.

"Chauncey," she said, nodding at the owl. "I don't have many visitors, Freddy, but when I do, Chauncey always flits over to his cage and gives them the eye. With Mr. FitzDuncan, he's stayed on his perch and his eyes are closed. He feels comfortable. Tea will be ready soon. How is your head?"

I realized, with a bit of surprise, the ache in my head had nearly vanished. "Much better. Thank you."

The kettle started to whistle and she went to tend it. I turned to Freddy and raised an eyebrow. He shrugged in response, as though to say, 'I don't understand any more than you do.'

Lucy came back in with a tray. She arranged the cups, lifted the lid on the teapot to see if it had steeped enough, then began to pour. The tea had a pleasant smell.

"Milk? Sugar?" she asked.

Freddy and I shook our heads. She handed us our cups, then took her own and seated herself on a low stool. She lifted the cup up and took a deep sniff before having a sip.

"Why do you want to know about the dark arts?" she asked me.

I almost began blurting out the whole story before remembering myself. "Milady, I must request that you keep what I'm about to tell you in the strictest confidence."

I'd never been embarrassed to make that request before now. Somehow, before I even asked, I knew Lucy would never betray my trust. My asking made me feel cheap.

"Of course," she responded lightly. She looked at me with curiosity. "You feel awkward," she observed.

I cleared my throat, hoping to settle my thoughts. "Yes," I admitted. "Discretion is very important to me, but I shouldn't have made that request."

"Why not?" Freddy asked.

"Because I have a feeling your cousin is someone whom I can trust unreservedly. I don't know why I feel that way, but it's very strong."

"You *can* trust me, Casimir FitzDuncan," she said.

Somehow I also sensed from her tone that I was forgiven. My embarrassment faded quickly. Unbidden, a smile appeared on my face. I don't know why it pleased me so much to be back in the good graces of this woman I'd just met.

"Now, why do you need to know about the dark arts?" she asked again.

I explained the whole story. As soon as I mentioned the Viscount, she snorted and rolled her eyes. I finally reached Freddy's idea that du Pais might be waiting for a special day to do something with Miss Traval, in order to bind himself to the Lord of the Seven Hells and increase his power.

Lucy took a sip of her tea and then placed the cup and saucer on the tray. "Where to begin?" she mused. She took a deep breath. "There is a new moon coming in three days. It will be the second new moon of the month. That's a rare occurrence and has significance for practitioners of the dark arts. So, the third night from now would be the time he would choose if that is his object—with the ceremony to conclude at midnight. It will certainly bind him to the Lord of the Seven Hells but won't increase his ability."

"How do you know?" Freddy asked.

"There hasn't been any talent in the du Pais clan for more than seven generations," she replied, shaking her head with a smile. "There has to be some innate ability in order for any ritual to work. Bergeron has none."

"Are you sure?" Freddy inquired. "I've heard he can do things."

"Conjuror's tricks," she said dismissively. "Something he probably learned as a boy at home in order to cover up that fact that he has no real talent."

"You're certain?" I asked.

"I've been introduced to the man," she answered. "I've perceived his aura. He has no magical ability of any kind."

"Are the dark arts real?" I inquired.

"Certainly," she responded. "They are nothing to be taken lightly. Fortunately for all of us, there is no one with any talent in the dark arts remaining in any aristocratic family. Those few with talent are scattered out in the countryside. I don't know whether any of them performed the ritual to awaken their full power. That information is closely guarded and unlikely to be available to country folk."

"Did Nan have talent?" Freddy asked.

Lucy laughed. "Yes, but not in the dark arts. That frustrated Grand-Nan tremendously. She blamed it on not being taught properly when she was growing up. That's why she insisted on taking over my upbringing. She tried everything she could to try to convert my talent into an affinity for the dark arts. It didn't work, much to her despair."

"About du Pais," I said, trying to get back to what I needed to know. "Does he know that whatever ritual he performs will be unsuccessful?"

"I can't say," Lucy replied. "It depends on what he believes and whether he is deluding himself. His family might have taught him that the parlor tricks he learned are manifestations of genuine talent instead of fakery to cover up its absence. He might believe the rituals will work. I doubt it, though. Bergeron's aura shows he is deeply cynical."

"If he knows it won't work," Freddy interjected, "why would he go through with it?"

"Because he has a sick mind," I guessed.

Turning to Lucy, I asked, "Where would he conduct this ceremony? Is there a particular location that would have more meaning?"

"I guess that depends on whether he believes it will work," she said. "If he believes he can indeed kindle his powers, then an altar in a temple of the Three Major Gods would be most pleasing to the Lord of the Seven Hells. Since the Three Major Gods cast him down, desecrating one of their altars would provide him the greatest satisfaction."

"I hate to ask, milady," I said to Lucy. "Do you have any idea what sort of ritual du Pais has planned?"

"Please. Call me Lucy. Now, if he believes the ritual will work, he would probably begin with a black marriage. That's a perversion of the normal marriage ceremony, with all the prayers offered to the Lord of the Seven Hells instead of the three Major and nine Minor Gods. He would then consummate the marriage on the altar. After that, he will slit her throat, allowing her blood to desecrate everything it touches."

Freddy's face showed great distaste. Lucy noticed. She continued.

"For the ritual to work, she must submit to this willingly. Now, no one in her right mind would ever agree to this perversion, so he will likely force Miss Traval to drink a concoction beforehand. It will make her compliant. Whatever he gives her will be powerful enough to remove her free will, but not so powerful that it will make her lose consciousness."

"Where would he get something like this?" I asked.

"Any herbalist," she responded. "The chief ingredient comes from poppies. In small doses, it's a powerful pain-killer. In slightly larger doses, it will do exactly what he wants. He merely has to take care not to give her too much. I would guess that somewhere in his family papers, there's a chart showing what the proper dose would be, depending on a person's weight."

"How do you know all this?" Freddy asked incredulously.

"Grand-Nan went over it with me many times," she explained. "She wanted me to know exactly what I needed to do for my own ritual of awakening. In particular, she stressed the proper dosage of the potion since my 'husband' would need to be able to maintain enough of an erection so I could lose my virginity. That's how I know that Bergeron probably has a chart. Grand-Nan had one."

Curious, I asked, "Do you still have it?"

"I know where all of Grand-Nan's books and papers are," she replied. "They're locked in a lead-lined trunk, which I buried behind the barn, back home."

I looked at her with a dubious expression.

"Spellbooks, written by hand, carry an aura of their own," she explained to me. "Grand-Nan's books have a malevolent aura. When you put them all together in a group, even people like Freddy, who have no talent whatsoever, would feel uncomfortable. You can tell where I buried the trunk. It's in the middle of the area of grass where the animals won't go. I think being surrounded by those books all her life is what made Grand-Nan so unpleasant."

"You said I have no magical talent," Freddy responded. "Why didn't you mention Caz, too? Just being polite?"

Lucy laughed. "Freddy, you, of all people, know that I'm only polite when I absolutely must be. Sometimes, not even then."

I noticed she did not answer Freddy's question.

"So, three nights from now, du Pais will be conducting his ceremony. He'll probably choose a temple to the Three Major Gods. He will time it to conclude at midnight," I summarized. "*If* he is the one who kidnapped the girl. Thank you, Lucy. That's more information than I had before our visit."

"You are most welcome, Caz," she replied. "Can I interest you gentlemen in dinner?"

"Sadly, we ate before we arrived. It was a most unfashionable hour," Freddy explained. "Caz's stomach complained. He'd missed breakfast and lunch."

"Too bad," she commented.

"Perhaps you could join us," I blurted. "Freddy promised his man, Theo, that we would spend the evening gambling, drinking to excess and — " I thought better of completing the sentence.

"There's an inn a couple of doors away," she said. "You can feed me and I can watch the two of you begin the excessive drinking. There's no gambling in that establishment, however."

"The extended pleasure of your company, cousin Lucy, along with the rap to the head he took last night, probably has Caz feeling half-drunk already. We would be delighted to have you join us for a time."

# 3

Contrary to what we promised Theo, I had no desire to make it a long night. Lucy joined us for dinner. She ate while Freddy and I contented ourselves with a glass of wine and a bit of bread and cheese. I have to admit, I found Lucy enchanting. She was very direct, beautiful (to my eyes, at any rate), and quick-witted. It was a most enjoyable time, and I was sad when we escorted her back to her shop.

"Where to?" Freddy asked after Lucy went in.

"I hate to make a liar of you to Theo," I said, "but I would enjoy making it an early night. Do you mind?"

"Not at all," Freddy said agreeably.

As we walked through the darkness, I thought about our evening. I had enjoyed meeting Lucy. I found her damnably attractive and briefly entertained the idea of seeing more of her. I caught myself quickly and scolded myself for having such thoughts. Her father was the Duke of Gulick. Though her family disapproved of her engaging in trade, that displeasure would pale in comparison to what she would face if they realized a bastard was paying court to her. I was also distressed to learn we had little time to unravel this mess. With today spent, we had tomorrow and the next day.

When we passed under a street lamp, Freddy noticed my cheerless expression. "It can't be that bad, Caz," he commented. "We've had a pleasant afternoon and evening. We got you fed, had a couple of glasses of wine with charming company, and learned what du Pais is probably going to do, if he's the kidnapper. I'd say a success on nearly all counts."

Freddy did always have a way of emphasizing the positive. I smiled in response. "I think I'm just worn out, Freddy. My day started much earlier and much less pleasantly. You're right, though. All's well that ends well."

We turned the corner. The bookseller was just ahead. Three men stepped out of the shadows.

"Oy, ya bastard," the one in the middle said.

Freddy and I stopped short of them.

"This don't concern the toff," the man said. "Run along now, Mr. Gentleman," he said to Freddy snidely.

To his credit, Freddy didn't move. I wasn't sure how much help he would be in the fight to come. In fact, I was fairly certain he would be a liability.

"That's a good idea, Freddy," I said. "Go find a member of the Watch. Tell him to bring some others since he'll need help to carry these three to the Palace of Justice. Hurry. One of them might end up bleeding in the street, and I'd rather not make too big of a mess."

At my urging, Freddy took a couple of steps to the side. That was good. With him out of the way, I had one less worry. I could see that the outer two of the trio were carrying cudgels. Their leader appeared unarmed, but I knew from experience he likely had a knife.

The men stepped closer as Freddy sidled away. They crowded me enough now that I couldn't draw my blade easily. I knew what I could do to gain that room, but I needed the men to come just a little closer. I had one advantage. Based on my appearance, these thugs undoubtedly thought I would fight like a gentleman.

"Don't worry. I'll be fine, Freddy," I said.

As I spoke, the trio took another half-step towards me. That was what I wanted. I lunged forward, grabbing the leader by the shoulders. I aimed my forehead for the bridge of his nose. I hit it, dead on. It made a most satisfactory sound. Even better, the destruction of the bones in his nose cushioned the impact for my forehead. The cudgels of his men fell on my shoulders. They hurt, but nothing to slow me down. As the one began to fall, I shoved him aside and stepped past quickly into open space, turning and drawing my blade as I did.

His two accomplices had only begun to react. They were smart enough to realize that the situation had changed dramatically. Instead of facing someone who would ineffectually resist the beating they were assigned to deliver, their leader was now lying in the street. His hands were clutched to his face, with blood pouring through his fingers while he moaned. Facing them was a grinning maniac, the sword in his hand gleaming in the dim light.

They did the sensible thing. They turned and ran. Freddy was still standing in the street, his mouth agape.

"Freddy," I said calmly, "please do go find a member of the Watch. I'll stay here and keep our friend company."

Freddy nodded and took off at a jog. My blade still drawn, I crouched down next to the moaning leader of the trio. His hands were still covering his ruined nose.

"So, 'friend,' why don't you tell me who sent you?" I asked politely.

"Fuck off, bastard," was his response.

26

"I don't like that answer," I stated. I smacked his hands with the flat of my blade, hard enough to drive them into his broken nose. That generated a yelp of pain.

"How did you know to find me?" I asked.

"I didn't," he replied. "They told me to teach a lesson to FitzDuncan the bastard. Tell him not to not to interfere with things don't concern him. Billy's from around here. He knows ya."

"Who sent you?"

The man rolled away from me to prevent me from smacking his face again. That didn't bother me. I stood and kicked him in the kidneys. That produced a new sound, sort of a strangled howl. I kicked him again in the same spot since the first one had felt so satisfying. I heard the same noise.

"You make some interesting sounds, 'friend.' But not the ones that would convince me to stop hurting you. Who sent you?"

"Fuck off," came his answer, though I must admit, it was not uttered with the same force and bravado as his earlier, similar responses.

I kicked him in the balls this time. That generated an 'oof' sound. Unfortunately, it also caused him to pass out. I saw the whites of his eyes in the dim light as they rolled up in his head.

"Damn," I muttered. I sheathed my sword.

Freddy came along a few minutes later. Two members of the Watch were huffing and puffing behind him. They stopped and looked at the unconscious man.

"Right," said the heftier of the two. "Go get a cart, Tommy."

The other one slumped his shoulders. "Where?" he asked.

"Any one of these shops that's got a cart lying around," the larger one answered, exasperated. "We borrow the cart, take this fella to a cell, then you return the cart to where you got it."

"Why do I have to do it?" the second one whined.

"Because I said so."

He waited for his partner to leave, then addressed Freddy. "Right, sur. I reckon we can take it from here. I thank you gentlemen for helping keep the streets safe."

I nodded and began to walk to the bookseller. Freddy caught up with me in a couple of steps. He tugged at my arm. As I turned, I saw the watchman cutting the fallen thug's money pouch from his belt. That wasn't why Freddy stopped me.

"I would feel more comfortable, Caz, if you spent the night at my place," he stated.

"I can lock my doors, Freddy," I responded.

"That won't be much help if they decide to set the place on fire," he countered.

I considered that then nodded. "Good point. As long as you promise

Theo won't try to kill me in my sleep."

"Theo is insulting, but not violent," Freddy explained. "He'll be quite upset to see you there in the morning, though."

"That gives me something to look forward to," I replied. "Let me get a couple of things."

Freddy came in with me. I lit a lamp at the top of the landing and gave it to him. I found another and lit it, carrying it with me as I found a small valise and threw what I would need into it. Within minutes, we were on our way.

When we arrived at Freddy's, we saw no sign of Theo, the grumpy manservant. Freddy showed me to his guest room. I undressed and climbed into bed, extinguishing the lamp.

It had been quite a day, I thought. I wondered who had sent the thugs to scare me off and, more importantly, why. The kidnapper was the obvious answer, but was it du Pais or someone else? I reviewed what we had discussed with Lucy.

In particular, I was stuck on the question of whether du Pais believed that performing the ritual would truly awaken some dark magical power. I'd had only a few encounters with the man, but he struck me as someone who would not entertain romantic illusions about magical powers. If he knew the ritual would not result in gaining power… That's when it occurred to me. The ritual *would* result in du Pais gaining power, but not of the magical kind.

If his friends participated in the ritual, and du Pais had arranged for there to be witnesses, then he would be able to manipulate them. It wouldn't be such a magnificent prize to gain control over that gang of sycophants and toadies. To have Albert, the Crown Prince, under his power… that was a different matter. If the king learned of Albert's involvement, it would cost Albert the throne. Albert would be lucky if he were merely exiled and Wim would inherit. Whether that would be such a bad thing was the last thought I remember before falling asleep.

I woke in the morning to the sound of Freddy whistling. I made myself presentable and went to find him. I caught up with him in the dining room.

"Good morning, Caz. Have a seat," he said. "Breakfast should be ready presently."

Almost on cue, Theo came in, bearing two plates with eggs, sausage and toast. He set one down in front of Freddy and the other in front of me. Freddy then took the plates and switched them.

"Theo, if I find anything unpleasant on this plate you served to my guest, then by all the Majors and Minors, I swear I will have you sacked," he said.

Freddy picked up his fork and began to look under the eggs. Theo whisked the plate away from him. Freddy shook his head.

"Rat droppings," he explained. "Better check yours, too."

I looked. I found nothing unusual hidden under the food on my plate. Freddy laughed and told me to eat and not wait.

"Did you learn what you needed to?" he asked.

"Not everything," I replied, "but I know a great deal more than I did yesterday. Thank you. Your cousin Lucy was most helpful."

"What are we doing today?" he asked.

"*We* aren't doing anything," I answered. "The last thing in the world I want would be for your name to be dragged into this mess. I have some inquiries to make."

"But this is the most interesting thing that has come my way in ages," he protested. "And you don't have much time."

"What would you be doing today, normally?" I asked.

"I'd get dressed," he began. "I'd go to the Equestrian Club and likely stay until lunch. Play some cards. If there was no one to play cards with, probably go for a ride. Then I'd come home, change, and head out to the Metropolitan Club for the afternoon. I generally find a card game there. Then, dinner, home and bed."

"I want you to do exactly that," I said. "Except meet me here for dinner."

"But that's boring," he complained.

"Perhaps… but perhaps not," I counseled. "You know a great deal more about certain things today than you did yesterday. I can't go to either of those clubs unless I'm someone's guest. Even when I'm there, most people won't talk to me. But you, dear Freddy—people talk to you. They confide in you. I'll bet you hear something every week that would rock the kingdom if it were made public."

"Well, yes," Freddy said, with a certain smugness, as my sweet-talking found fertile ground between his ears.

"There's a certain topic on which we'd like more information—information that only you can obtain. Fortunately, you are subtle enough that you would never let anyone know where your interest lies. You'll merely keep your ears open and when we see one another tonight, you'll know more than we do now. Plus, by keeping your distance from me, you avoid suspicion. That makes you even more valuable."

"Ah," Freddy said, laying his finger aside his nose, signifying he understood his role. "I understand. You'll be staying again tonight?"

"I think it would be best," I answered. "Until we are past this whole thing if you don't mind."

I hated feeling as though I were manipulating Freddy but reasoned to myself that I wasn't entirely dishonest. It was entirely possible that he might overhear someone talking about what du Pais and his friends were doing. Freddy certainly enjoyed the ability to go places where I could not.

"Caz, you are welcome any time, despite how Theo might treat you."

After finishing breakfast, I dressed, then took my leave. I went back to my rooms, carrying my valise. Finding the building still standing and the door still locked reassured me. I packed a fresh change of clothes but left the bag by the door.

On the street again, I headed to the Palace of Justice to see Sir Oliver West. I took a hackney to save time. In particular, I wanted to know if a ransom demand had been made and learn more from the man who accosted me last night. It was still early before judicial proceedings began for the day, so I had every confidence the man was still nestled safely in the bosom of the cells.

I had the cabbie drop me at the entrance to the administrative wing and not the main entrance. A scribe was seated at the end of the hall from the entrance door. He looked at me expectantly as I approached.

"Casimir FitzDuncan, to pay his respects to Sir Oliver West, please," I instructed him.

He nodded in confirmation, rose, and went through the double doors behind his station. I entertained myself by examining the portraits of Sir Oliver's predecessors hung on the walls of the entrance hall. Most of them looked like typical men of means in the city, but there was one I particularly liked. He had a patch over his left eye, a thin, hooked nose, and a scar on his forehead that angled down and disappeared under the eye patch. Of all of them, he was the only one I think I would have liked to meet.

The scribe returned and collected me. He led me to the double doors, then asked if I knew where Sir Oliver's office was. When I nodded, he sent me through and closed the doors behind me. I went up the stairs to the left and turned right at the top. When I reached his door, I knocked.

"Enter," he called.

"Hello, Ollie," I greeted him.

"Caz," he replied flatly.

"I was hoping you and I could go visit one of your new residents. A young man with a broken nose who arrived last night."

Sir Oliver frowned. It made deep creases on both sides of his mouth. He shook his head.

"I'm afraid he is no longer a resident of the Palace of Justice," he stated.

"How?" I asked, surprised. "Proceedings don't start for almost another hour!"

"A solicitor appeared with a habeas writ early this morning," he explained. "We had to release him."

"Huh!" I grunted. I stood in thought. After reflection, I said, "That's useful information, Ollie. Thank you. Has there been a demand for ransom presented to Traval?"

"Not yet."

I nodded and turned to leave. "Are you making any progress, Caz?" he asked.

"Indirectly, Ollie. Only indirectly," I said. As I exited, I cautioned, "Your people will probably come across his body before nightfall."

"Whose?"

"Broken nose."

The purpose of my visit was to quiz the man to learn who sent me after me. What Sir Oliver shared gave me more information than the thug could. The ruffian probably had no idea who had made the request to attack me. He was an underling, merely following orders he'd been given. I would then have needed to climb a few rungs up the ladder of his gang to learn where the request originated.

What Sir Oliver told me eliminated the need for that. The orders came from someone who had the clout to have a judicial writ issued shortly after the sun came up. There were few people in the kingdom who could make that happen. Associated with the mess I was currently untangling; I could think of only one. He lived in the castle and was a friend of the Viscount.

Upon leaving the Palace of Justice, I decided it was time to call upon the missing girl's father. I had no firm idea where his offices were, but a merchant of his type would be within a block or two of the wharves. As it was still early and I had plenty of time, I decided to walk. While I walked, the temperature dropped on this autumn day, making me wish I'd worn a thicker jacket.

After living in the city of Aquileia for the last three years, there were certain neighborhoods I could identify from smell alone. Baker Street was one of the most pleasant. The Wharf District was on the other end of the spectrum. The dominant odors were of sewage and rotted fish. Closer to the river's mouth, the sewage smell held sway. Further away from the river, the aroma of dead fish came to the fore. I've heard that some become accustomed to the stench. They say that every port has its own unique odor, and that sailors can tell them apart—able to identify the smell of 'home.' I have no wish to become that familiar with the smell.

I reached the water's edge. I stopped a fishmonger pushing her cart and asked her where Traval had his office. She gave me a gap-toothed look, then jabbed her thumb over her shoulder. I gave her a quarter-florin. She cackled. I hope that was her happy sound.

His office was one block over and one block away from the water. As I'd walked to this part of the city, I'd thought about how to approach Mr. Herbert Traval. He knew his daughter had planned to see me. It was he who informed the Viscount. I'm certain the Viscount had told him nothing complimentary about me. Indeed, I would not be surprised if Bergeron du Pais blamed me for the daughter's disappearance.

Somehow, I needed to convince Traval that du Pais was not his ally. I doubted I could accomplish that in a single visit. I expected he would throw me out of his offices this time. He would probably throw me out the second time, too. I hoped when I returned the third time, he would equate my persistence with sincerity and begin to listen to me.

I entered his offices. A thin-faced older man, wearing a green visor and spectacles, put his quill down and looked at me. "My name is Casimir FitzDuncan. I'd like to speak with Mr. Traval."

"Is he expecting you?" he asked, in a querulous voice that entirely suited his appearance.

"No, but it's a matter of some importance," I replied.

The old man sniffed dismissively, clearly not believing there was any importance to my visit. He rose slowly, looking at me skeptically. He left through the door behind him, shutting it firmly.

After a brief wait, he returned. He grinned at me. He displayed far too much amusement for this to be a pleasant outcome for me.

"Someone will be with you presently," he said.

Two barrel-chested men, carrying short pieces of wood that looked like cudgels (I later learned they are called belaying pins) came through the door behind him. Two others, equally imposing and similarly armed, entered the door to the street behind me. I slipped sideways, trying to get my back to a wall. One of them tried to clamp my shoulder with his hand, but I dipped under it.

"Mr. Traval don't want to see you," the old man said in a thin, reedy voice.

"I guessed that," I replied. "Even so, I have something important to tell him."

"He don't want to hear anything from you," the old man said.

He nodded to the others. The two closest to me seized my upper arms and lifted me so my feet no longer touched the ground. That was impressive. I'm not small and weighed nearly 14 stone. One of the other two opened the door to the street. The men holding my arms threw me out. I flew over the steps and staggered upon landing. I was thankful my sword had not been tangled in my legs, or I would have fallen in a heap.

When I collected myself, I shouted, "I know he doesn't believe this, but I'm trying to help him."

The door shut. Not with a slam, but solidly. I did not linger in front of the building. I decided to walk around the block and see what other ways I might find into the building. On the other side, there were doors large enough to fit a wagon. They were shut and locked. I would need to bring a prybar with me the next time.

I kicked myself for not asking Sir Oliver where Traval lived. I still needed to learn whether Miss Traval had a paramour who would have tried to rescue her from this ill-omened marriage. Despite my focus on Bergeron du Pais, I still had not ruled out that possibility. Her mother might not have the same feelings about the marriage contract as her father.

I walked back to the center of the city. It was uphill. Within minutes, I no longer felt chilly. My destination was the financial district. I wanted to learn more about du Pais's debt. I would be calling upon the man Freddy had referred to me after I won back Freddy's ring. I had helped this man retrieve some compromising letters. He was not in the business of personal loans, but he should be able to point me in the right direction. He now took care of my money.

When I reached his offices, I was ushered in without difficulty. Pierre Luin greeted me warmly. When I explained what I was seeking, he frowned.

"Do you know who lent the money to du Pais?" I asked.

"You won't find the people who engage in that sort of lending here in the financial district," he cautioned. "People like those are predators."

"Do you know who they are?"

"Yes. Before I give you their names, though, I would ask you to consider whether contacting these men could possibly help you. Dealing with them is like trying to juggle a ball of tar. It sticks to you so you can't get rid of it. Everywhere it touches, it leaves a stain. Du Pais will learn this unpleasant fact. Even if he repays the money, he will never be free of them."

"If he is unable to repay them?" I asked.

"If they can find a way to use him to get their money back, they'll keep him alive. If they decide he is of no further use to them, he will die unpleasantly, in a way that will send a message to other debtors," Pierre said.

After considering, I promised Pierre I would keep what he said in mind. I asked him to write the names on a piece of paper and seal it. I would take the paper. If I decided I did not need to contact these men, I would burn it, unopened.

I left his office with the paper in my pocket. It was now midday. I stopped in a tavern I knew and had a bowl of stew. While I ate, I thought about Pierre's concerns.

I kept reaching the same conclusion. I would not need to contact these people. It would be better to remain as unknown to them as possible.

After finishing my lunch, I paid and entered the street. I realized I was only two blocks away from Lucy's shop. Though my logical brain told me to keep my distance, my feet carried me halfway there. When I realized what I had done, it perplexed me. It wasn't as though I had been lost in thought and wandered aimlessly. I'd been vigorously talking myself out of going to see her while my feet took me closer.

Having already covered half the distance, against my better judgment, I gave in and went the rest of the way. When I opened the door to her shop, the bell jingled. Lucy was sitting on a high stool facing the door as though she had been waiting for me. She had a broad smile.

"Nice to see you again, Casimir FitzDuncan," she greeted.

"And you, as well, Lady… uh… ah… I'm afraid you have me at a disadvantage, milady. I never asked Freddy what your proper title is."

She slid off the stool and crossed to me, laying her hand on my arm. She looked at me, smiling. "For my friends, the proper form of address is…

Lucy," she teased.

"My friends call me Caz," I replied.

"I know. What brings you here today, Caz?"

Why did I come? I didn't really understand myself. So I wouldn't seem entirely dull-witted, I gave her a flippant answer. "My feet. My feet brought me here."

She laughed. Her laugh had almost the same pleasant timber as the bell on her door. It was slightly different but just as sweet-sounding. I did not feel she was laughing at the quality of my quip. She was laughing because she knew I had no idea why I'd come.

"You didn't come seeking my advice on what you've learned about the Viscount?" she asked.

She was leading me by the hand back to her stool. She switched hands as she hopped back on it. She nodded at the stool next to her. She did not let go of my hand. Her fingers were cool and dry. I was acutely conscious of her touch.

"That must have been the reason," I said, though who knows if I'd been thinking that.

"So," she batted her eyelashes at me, "are you going to tell me?"

Her eyes, the palest blue I'd ever seen, were twinkling. I had always thought that a 'twinkle in the eye' was just an expression, but, damme, her eyes were twinkling. She had a spray of freckles across the bridge of her nose and across her upper cheeks. Her smile brought out dimples below the freckles.

"Well, Caz?"

"Oh! Right," I said. I wanted to shake my head like a wet dog. "When I had a chance to think things through, after what you shared with us last evening, I reached a different conclusion."

"Go on."

"If Bergeron abducted the girl—which is looking more likely since there has not been a request for ransom—he doesn't believe the ritual will give him magical power. If it does, he'd certainly welcome it, but that isn't his priority. What du Pais hopes to gain from this, in addition to the million ducats from the girl's father, is power over the others in that group. If he gets the others to participate in the ritual and has witnesses hidden in the shadows, he can threaten to ruin all of them. He will have an iron grip on Albert. If the king found out Albert did something like this — "

Lucy adopted a more sober expression. "How will he convince the others to take part?" she asked.

"He undoubtedly told them their participation would grant them some magical power. If they aren't motivated by that, he might use the same tincture or potion you described. He would use the same dose that your grandmother would have given the man in the ritual she planned for you—

enough to take away their free will while still leaving them the ability to, uh, perform."

"That makes sense," she said, nodding. "It makes far more sense than what we were thinking last night."

"It also changes the location," I added.

Lucy raised her eyebrows in a questioning response.

"If he knows the ritual won't succeed in giving him magical power, then there is no need to desecrate a temple. Since his primary target is Albert, he will hold the ritual in the place that is most damning to Albert—somewhere in the castle."

"You're brilliant, Caz," she murmured. "I'm convinced you're right."

"*If* du Pais is the one who did this," I qualified. "A true kidnapper could still be the culprit, but so far, he has not made any demands. There's another possibility that I haven't been able to explore. If Miss Traval already had a suitor who knew about her predicament, he might have abducted her — "

"To save her," Lucy finished. "And to elope. Oh, I hope it turns out to be that. That's so much more pleasant than what you've been thinking."

# 4

"Yes, well, I need to run that information down tomorrow. I tried to talk to her father today and was thrown out of his office."

"Find her mother," Lucy suggested.

"I agree. Now, if pursuing du Pais is the correct choice, I'm still at a dead end," I muttered. "I don't know the first thing about the castle. I don't know what rooms it includes or how they connect or anything. I've never been in it and I'll certainly never be invited in. I also don't know where Miss Traval is. That's another significant problem."

"I'm sure we know someone who is familiar with the castle. If I don't, Freddy does. Where is Freddy, by the way?"

"I feel bad about involving Freddy as much as I have," I confessed. "And you, for that matter. I sent Freddy off on his usual rounds of the Equestrian Club and Metropolitan Club, with instructions to keep his ears wide open for any information that could help us."

"He'll be gone all day," she said with a giggle. "If only to stay away from Theo. Have you met Theo yet?"

"I've had the pleasure," I joked. "He tried to serve me rat droppings in my breakfast this morning."

Lucy burst out laughing. Then she clapped her hand over her mouth, fearing that I might not see the humor. When I chuckled as well, she relaxed.

"You had breakfast with Freddy?"

"I spent the night." I explained to Lucy about the men who accosted us as we neared my lodging and Freddy's insistence that I spend the night. I also told her about stopping by the Palace of Justice that morning to find that the scoundrel had been released by a judicial writ.

"Is that significant?" she asked.

"Waking a judge up in the morning and getting him to write out a document to free a common criminal is not something that just anyone can do," I explained. "The only person I can think of, who has that kind of influence, is Albert."

"If this is aimed at Albert, he seems to be a willing victim, don't you think?" she suggested.

I considered her point. It troubled me. This was not the time or the place to get into that discussion. I shrugged my shoulders as an answer.

"Are you spending the night at Freddy's again?" she asked.

I nodded.

"Check your bed," she warned.

A disgusted laugh escaped from my throat as I contemplated what Theo might do. Her more musical laugh was counterpoint to mine. I shook my head.

"A snake," I suggested. "Poisonous, of course."

"Of course," she agreed. "A scorpion," she added.

"More rat droppings," I offered.

"A dead rat. In the pillowcase," she countered. "And a dead fish in the sheets."

I grimaced while laughing. Lucy began laughing harder. That fed my laughter. She withdrew her hand from mine as she needed to clutch her side. Our fit of hysterics finally subsided.

"Hooooo," she gasped, gaining control of herself. She reached and took my hand in hers again.

"Speaking of which," I said, "I should warn the proprietor of the shop where my rooms are about the risk. These people know where I live. They've tried to frighten me away already. Freddy suggested they will try to burn it down and he might be right."

I stood to leave. Lucy stood also, still holding my hand. She was looking up at me. The desire to kiss her lips seized me. I fought it off and gave her a kiss on the cheek instead. Even that was far too forward, given our relative stations in life. It would have been entirely proper for her to slap my face.

"I apologize, milady," I quickly stammered. "That was inappropriate of me."

I was sure I had overstepped, but her expression did not convey any sense of being insulted. She looked slightly disappointed. That puzzled me. I backed away as quickly as I could without appearing to stumble and run. I put my hand on the door latch.

"Caz," she called softly, "I took no offense."

She was smiling, her expression warm. I didn't know how to respond, so I nodded. I opened the door and slipped through.

As I walked away, I wanted to hit myself in the head for being so stupid. High-born ladies, even those who engaged in trade, did not receive kisses from bastards like me. I was sure Freddy would hear about it and equally certain it would end our friendship. I cursed myself for my impulsiveness.

My life was complicated enough at the moment. I had just made it worse.

Lost in these thoughts, chastising myself, I never knew what hit me. The next thing I knew, a man whose breath reeked of garlic was leaning over me, asking me a question. His voice, and the sounds of activity nearby, seemed very distant, as though passing through a thick layer of wool. I wondered where I was briefly before realizing I was flat on my back, lying in the street.

"Sur," garlic breath asked, "are you alright?"

I was confused and disoriented. I most definitely was not 'alright.' Instead of answering the man's question, I asked, "What happened?"

"You was robbed, sur. The old smash and grab it was. The one conked you in the head and one of the others grabbed your money and all three of 'em ran off, quick as lightning."

I could now feel where they'd hit me. At least it wasn't the same spot as before. I started to sit up. The man gave me a hand. Sitting upright caused a wave of dizziness. I waited for it to pass. I looked around slowly and carefully, not wanting to make my head spin again. I saw I was only about a block away from the bookseller's. There were a few people standing nearby who were looking at me with curiosity.

"Can you give me a hand up, friend?" I asked.

"Sure," garlic breath responded.

He clasped my hand with our thumbs interlocked and pulled me to my feet. There was a horse rail a few steps over, and I nodded slightly in its direction. With his hand holding my upper arm firmly, he guided me to it. I was able to rest my butt on it to keep from keeling over.

"Thanks, friend. I'd offer to reward you for your help, but I guess I'm out of funds."

"That's not necessary, sur," he said. "Can I help you get somewhere?"

"I live just down the block," I explained. "I think I can make it. I just need to take a minute. Get my wits again."

"That's fine, sur. If you're sure you don't need my help, I'll be on my way."

"I'm sure. And thank you."

He knuckled his forelock and turned, walking away. Gazing around, no one was paying attention to me any longer. Life on the street had returned to its normal hustle and bustle. I looked down at my clothes. Dirty, from landing in the street, but not as bad as the day before. Majors and Minors, I thought, was that only yesterday?

After a bit, I decided to head for the shop. My first few steps were wobbly. I stopped and leaned against a wall, then pushed off again. I made it to the shop. Lyle was there. I crooked my finger at him through the window, indicating I'd like to talk. I stepped away from the window and tucked myself next to the door, where the assistants wouldn't see me. Lyle came out presently as though he were just getting some fresh air. He saw me but gave no indication of it.

"Lyle," I said. "I'm involved in a particularly messy piece of business. In the last 24 hours, they have attacked me in the street twice. Both times it was close to here. They obviously know where I live and are trying to frighten me off. I fear they might escalate things. They could set fire to the place, thinking they'll catch me inside. You might want to have the assistants spend the night for the next two days to make sure they don't succeed. They can stay in my rooms. I'll be elsewhere."

Lyle didn't say a word in response. He merely stretched and took a deep breath, getting fresh air. He turned and went back inside.

I went to the alley and unlocked my door. After stripping off my dirty clothes, I put them in the hamper for Placida. Then I pulled out my strongbox and retrieved an old money pouch, filling it with about ten ducats in smaller coins. My head was pounding again. I resolved to go to an herbalist and get some of the bark that Lucy had given me the day before. I also needed a new money pouch. The one I'd just filled was scuffed and worn.

My bed was tempting me. I wanted to sleep but didn't have time. I needed to keep moving. Dressed in clean clothing, I sat and pondered my next step. Briefly, I considered taking my prybar and going to confront Traval. I decided I didn't have the energy.

Despite my intention to move along, sleep captured me. I had a dream that was bizarre. It was one of those dreams that was so strange that you realized it was a dream and you should wake up. I tried to wake myself but could not. I was in a room lit by torches. Lucy was naked and spread on an altar. She was grinning with a lustful expression. Theo, du Pais, Albert, the old man from Traval's office, the bloody-nosed thug and a line of others, dressed in black robes, were lined up to violate her. I was hung on the wall by my wrists. My throat was cut and blood was pouring forth, but I was still alive and conscious. Freddy appeared in front of me. My blood was spurting onto his chest. He wagged his finger at me, saying, "I will never forgive you, Caz." Lucy looked at me and laughed derisively. "You will never have me," she said. I looked to the side and saw Julienne Traval hanging on the wall next to me, her throat also cut. "This is all your fault," she stated. At the head of the altar, I saw Sir Oliver West. He was shaking his head in dismay. He looked up at me. "Just as I predicted," he stated.

With this, I was finally able to wrestle my way out of the dream. I woke, panting and sweating. Unlike most of my dreams, of which I remember only small fragments (if I remember them at all), this one was vivid in my mind. Looking at the window, I could tell the day had worn on. I realized I should go find Freddy to learn what he might have heard. I hoped the herbalist shop nearby was still open since my head was pounding. I took my valise and left. I was two steps in the alley before I remembered to lock my door.

I was in luck. The herbalist was still open. When I asked for the bark that cures headaches, she knew exactly what I wanted. I purchased some and chewed it as I walked to Freddy's.

I rang the bell. Theo answered the door. He sneered at me.

"Is Lord Rawlinsford in?" I asked politely.

As he did yesterday, Theo said, "I'll see."

Theo did not move. He did not call out to announce a visitor. He stood there motionless, with his sneer.

"Freddy?" I called.

"Come in, Caz," he replied. "Don't mind Theo."

I decided I *did* mind Theo. Instead of squirming past him, as I did yesterday, I lowered my shoulder and drove it into his gut. That staggered him back with an 'oof.' I pressed forward with my hand on his chest. When his back hit the wall, I slid my hand up to his throat and lifted.

"Theo," I said grimly but gently. "I've had a bad day. I would advise you not to test my patience and good nature further. My patience, especially with you, is exhausted, and my good nature is not going to return for several days. Do you understand?"

Theo's sneer was gone. He gave me a frightened nod. I released him.

"Good," I grunted. "And if you've prepared some sort of surprise in the bedclothes for me, I suggest you remove it before Lord Rawlinsford and I return from dinner, or else I'll cut your balls off."

Theo responded with another frightened nod. Satisfied that he understood, I took off my jacket and handed it to him. Unlike the day before, he held it normally. I then unbuckled my sword and gave that to him. Then I went to find Freddy. He was sprawled on a sofa, cradling a glass of sherry.

"I hope you had a more productive day than I did," he said.

I slumped into a chair. "Doubtful," I replied.

Freddy sat up, obviously expecting a report. I told him how I had been thwarted, stymied and then attacked. I left out the part when I went to see Lucy. I would share that over dinner once we'd left the house. Though I believed I had Theo cowed for now, if he learned I'd been inappropriate with Lucy, I feared he'd try to kill me in my sleep.

Freddy offered me a glass of sherry, but I declined. The bark I'd purchased from the herbalist had done its job, and my head no longer ached. Mixing alcohol with another crack to my head, though, did not seem to be a good idea.

"Perhaps my day *was* more productive than yours," Freddy joked.

"I hope so," I said.

"I overheard some gossip about du Pais. Everyone knows his betrothed has gone missing. Most seem to think she ran away to avoid marrying Bergeron. Sympathy is entirely on her side."

"As ours is," I commented.

Freddy continued, "Apparently, when the news of her abduction reached Bergeron, he took it quite calmly, saying something to the effect of, 'She'll turn up.' And Bergeron had a meeting with his creditors yesterday. According to what I heard, these men are not what we would consider financiers."

"I heard that, too," I said.

"Yes," Freddy agreed. "They are, by all accounts, dangerous men. No one knows what took place during the meeting, but the two men left. Apparently, Bergeron was able to satisfy them for now."

"You did have a more productive day," I confirmed.

"That's not all," Freddy added. "I also came home about fifty ducats to the good from my day at the tables."

I held my hands up in surrender. Freddy beamed. I waited for him to finish his glass. It was growing dark outside, so entirely logical to think about dinner. I mentioned it to him and he stood. When we reached the front hall, he was quite surprised to see my jacket hanging next to his, with my sword belt looped over, just as his was.

"Did you…?" he asked, pointing.

I shook my head.

"Huh," he muttered, not quite understanding why Theo had not dropped them on the floor as he usually did.

Freddy took me to an inn he liked. He recommended the pumpkin soup and the roast mutton. When the innkeeper had taken our orders, I swallowed hard and leaned in towards Freddy.

"I have something to tell you. This afternoon, before I was attacked, I went to see Lucy."

"So?"

"When I left, I'm afraid I wasn't entirely correct in my behavior. I gave her a kiss goodbye. On the cheek. I apologized to her and I'm apologizing to you. I will certainly understand if you feel I've betrayed your trust in me."

"How did this happen?" he asked in an angry tone.

My confession came spilling out. "I had been visiting a mutual acquaintance familiar with money-lending to ask him some questions about the situation du Pais is in. When I left his office, I realized I was close to Lucy's shop. I was telling myself it was a bad idea to pay her a visit, and somehow, I found my steps had carried me halfway there. That baffled me, but I decided not to fight it and went to her shop. She wanted to know what progress we'd made, and I gave her a summary. I told her you were kind enough to allow me to spend the night. She wanted to know if I'd met Theo. I shared with her how he had prepared my breakfast. She then wondered what sort of surprise he would have waiting in the bedclothes this evening. We traded ideas and laughed. By all the Majors and Minors, Freddy, I haven't laughed that well in a long time. When I left, shortly after, I felt compelled to kiss her. As soon as I did, I realized I had overstepped my bounds badly. I apologized and departed. I'm sorry, Freddy."

"You kissed her," he said sternly. "On the cheek. Why not the lips? If you're going to engage in such impropriety, why not the lips?"

How could I tell him it took all of my will to bend my head away from her lips?

"I'm sorry, milord. I should leave now." I began to rise.

"Sit down," he commanded. "I'm not finished with you. Scoundrel!"

I sat down, my head bowed and my eyes closed. I was prepared for whatever tongue-lashing he would deliver. I was already sad about losing the best friend I had.

"How did she react to this violation?" he demanded.

"She looked disappointed. I'm sure my forwardness caused that. She told me as I left that she took no offense, but I know she was simply being polite."

I could not look at Freddy. I stared at the table. The server arrived then with our soup.

"Mmm," Freddy murmured. "Nothing I like better in the fall than pumpkin soup."

His voice had lost its harsh tone. I was confused. I looked up. Freddy had just spooned some soup into his mouth and had a big smile on his face as he swallowed. Seeing the blank look on my face, he began to laugh. His laughter grew until his whole body was shaking. The harder he laughed, the less sound came out and the more he shook.

"You're not offended?" I asked as he began to calm down.

Freddy shook his head. "You should have kissed her on the lips. It's marvelous."

It was my turn to look shocked.

"What?" he asked. "She's my second cousin. I could marry her if I wanted. It happened during a school break. Lucy wanted to know more about kissing and picked me as her practice partner. For two days, we kissed at every chance we could. After two days, with our lips chapped and swollen, she decided she'd learned what she wanted to know and that was the end of it."

"You're not mad at me?" I asked.

"Nope," he said, shoveling more soup into his mouth. "Hurry and eat your soup before it gets cold," he advised.

"But Freddy," I protested. "Her father is the Duke of Gulick and I'm a bas—"

"Caz, sometimes you think too much. What sort of things do you think Theo will put in your bed?" he asked, changing the subject.

"Tonight? Nothing."

"I find that hard to believe," Freddy commented. "I figure he's good for more rat droppings, at least."

I shook my head. "I believe Theo and I have come to an understanding."

"Really?" Freddy commented between mouthfuls of soup. "What sort of understanding?"

"I threatened to cut his balls off if he did," I answered calmly, with a shrug.

I bent to my soup. It was delicious. I hurried to catch up to Freddy, who had paused from eating to laugh again until his face turned red.

"That explains why he hung up your jacket," he said.

When I finished my soup, I asked, "Freddy, about your cousin — "

"Caz, let whatever happens, happen. We can talk about it some other time. I'm confident that Lucy would not allow you to take any liberties that she wouldn't grant freely. That's all I'll say for now."

"Can you at least tell me what her title is, so I can address her properly?" I requested.

"Did you ask her?"

"Yes."

"What did she say?"

"Lucy."

Freddy laughed again. "Her formal title is Lady Darling, after one of the minor holdings in the Gulick territory. She always thought that was far too precious, so naturally, we teased her as much as possible by calling her Lady Darling at every opportunity."

"Of course."

"So, Caz, what obstacles remain?"

I realized I had not shared my thoughts with Freddy regarding what I now believed du Pais' aim was. I reviewed everything with him, beginning with our attacker being released from the Palace of Justice before I'd arrived first thing in the morning. Freddy agreed with me that Albert was proving to be a willing victim. I lamented my lack of knowledge regarding the castle. Just then, our mutton arrived.

"Sir Oliver," Freddy said before shoving the first bite in his mouth.

"What about him?" I asked.

Freddy held up a finger, telling me to wait for his answer. When he swallowed, he explained. "As Principal of the Watch, it's Sir Oliver's job to know every nook in the castle. You didn't ask him?"

I shook my head. "I was distracted by learning that there has been no demand for ransom and that our attacker was already free."

"Go back and ask him. What else?"

"I'd like to convince Traval about what is happening and about my belief that du Pais has no intention of helping steer business his way. I don't think I'll be able to see him, though. I need to find out whether Miss Traval had another suitor who might have staged the abduction in order to elope with her and prevent the marriage to the Viscount. I haven't even begun to look into that."

"Finally, I need to find the girl before this thing happens tomorrow night. If I can't find her, then I need to know where it will take place and figure out a way to get in there. I need to develop plans for how to deal with the situation if I'm not able to solve the other problems.

"All that depends on du Pais being the one driving this. If she was kidnapped by someone else, then we have more time to untangle this mess. If another suitor eloped with her, or her friends are trying to save her, then my job—our job—is finished. There would be no ritual and du Pais would have no more power over Albert and the others than he does now. The Viscount would get his money, and Traval would lose a million ducats. It would serve him right for being greedy and selling his daughter."

Freddy finished chewing his bite of mutton. "If her abduction was staged, and she eloped, why have you been attacked?"

"Because du Pais thinks I helped arrange it."

Freddy shook his head. "If she elopes, he still gets the million, right?"

"Yes."

"Then why on earth would he want to punish you?"

"Remember when you tried to introduce us at the races, and he pretended not to hear you?"

Freddy nodded.

"He would punish me for daring to interfere in the affairs of my betters," I stated.

Freddy cocked his head, considering that. "A bit thin, if you ask me," he said. "But it's not hard to see du Pais adopting that position."

"So, tomorrow it's back to the Palace of Justice to meet with Sir Oliver and learn where in the castle du Pais would conduct this ritual if it's him. I also need to obtain Madam Traval's address and call upon her. If she doesn't know of any other suitors or won't discuss them, we should try to get from her the names of some of Miss Traval's friends and interview them. By this time tomorrow, I'd like to be able to rule out elopement as a reason for her disappearance."

"If you can, then what will be left?" Freddy asked.

"A true kidnapping or du Pais. Every minute that passes without a request for ransom money convinces me more that Bergeron is responsible. It would be nice to know where Miss Traval is," I said. "With that information, we might be able to rescue her before things get messy. That would be best."

"Messy?" Freddy queried.

"If we still believe the Viscount is behind this, we somehow make our way into the castle. Then we find the room where this is taking place. We interrupt them. It's messy because we catch Albert in the thick of it," I stated.

"I see your point," Freddy conceded. "It would be messy. It also might not be a bad thing."

"Freddy, let's not even talk about that. Let's hope the girl eloped or that we can find her and rescue her. I don't know whether I can get inside the castle."

"Right," Freddy closed the subject. "What can I do to help? And don't say go to the club, or I'll punch you in the mouth."

"If I get Madam Traval's address, would you interview her? I think gentle Lord Rawlinsford might get much more information from her than that bastard, FitzDuncan. You'll probably have better luck with the girlfriends, too."

"What will you be doing?"

"I'll pretend to be Theo," I replied with a grin. "That gives me an excuse to listen."

# 5

When we returned that evening, I checked to see if Theo had left any surprise in the bedclothes for me. He hadn't. Freddy was amused.

"I'd still inspect your breakfast before eating it," he warned.

The next morning, we both inspected what Theo served us. I made a point of thanking Theo. Then I pulled him aside.

"In a few days, when Lord Rawlinsford and I have settled the matter in which we are currently involved, you may begin tormenting me again, if you'd like."

Theo did not react to my remark. His face remained blank and impassive. He turned and left the room without a word.

Freddy and I headed to the Palace of Justice. The same scribe was at the end of the entrance hall. I asked for Sir Oliver again.

He rose and went through the door. When he returned, he gestured us forward. Freddy and I climbed the stairs and turned to Sir Oliver's office. We found him seated behind his desk. When he saw Freddy, he leaped to his feet.

"Good morning, Lord Rawlinsford," he said, with a slight bob of his head.

Freddy didn't wait to be invited to sit. He just plunked himself down in the armchair nearest, sprawled, and crossed his legs. Perhaps, as Freddy told me the night before, I think too much. I doubt whether Sir Oliver would have stood if it had just been me. It was just another reminder to me of who I am.

"Hello, Ollie," I said to remind him I was also present.

I took the other armchair. That forced Sir Oliver to pull his chair from behind the desk to sit with us. I know it seems juvenile, my calling him by a nickname and not his title, then forcing him to rearrange himself. However misguided it was, I felt it helped even the scales. I'd learned back in boarding school that if I let people put me in my place, the place they would assign would not be one I would tolerate for long.

"What brings you here today, Lord Rawlinsford?" Sir Oliver said, ignoring my little jibe.

May all the Majors and Minors bless Freddy. He adopted his most patronizing tone, drawling, "I'm helping FitzDuncan with this Traval mess. I felt he should bring you up-to-date on what we've uncovered so far. Plus, there is information we need from you to wrap things up. Go ahead, FitzDuncan. Make your report."

The reason Freddy's haughty attitude pleased me is that it addressed the question of why he was here. It prevented Sir Oliver from asking any questions about it without seeming impertinent. It was not uncommon for people of Freddy's station to insert themselves into the business of others, regardless of whether their help was desired or even useful. His ordering me to make a report was a sign that he didn't understand the thing in which he had involved himself, but he was still planning on being in command.

I asked if there had been any word from kidnappers regarding ransom. Sir Oliver shook his head. Then I summarized the events of the last two days and what I had learned. I showed how the line of inquiry we had pursued so far seemed to point at Bergeron and my belief that a ceremony would take place within the castle that night. I neglected to reference our belief that du Pais had planned this to gain control over Albert. I emphasized the supernatural aspect instead. When I finished with that narrative, I mentioned it was still possible that Miss Traval had staged her own abduction in order to elope and avoid marrying the Viscount.

"I would like to speak with Madam Traval," Freddy stated when I finished. "Give FitzDuncan her address so we can attend to her this morning. I'm certain our inquiry will bear fruit and prove FitzDuncan's running around the city for the past two days has been a waste of time. If for some strange reason, our inquiry with Madam Traval does not immediately solve the issue, I would like you to provide FitzDuncan with detailed information about the rooms in the castle where du Pais would stage his silly ceremony. You will, of course, provide FitzDuncan and me with access to the castle in order to complete that assessment."

I could tell that Sir Oliver was not comfortable with Freddy's request for access to the castle. This is where Freddy's arrogant tone was pitch-perfect. It forced Sir Oliver into a position where disagreement might generate unpleasant consequences for him. Sir Oliver did the only thing he could.

He returned to his desk. He shuffled through some papers until he found what he was seeking. He scribbled some information on a sheet of paper.

"This is Madam Traval's address," he said. "After you have interviewed her, Lord Rawlinsford, would you be so kind as to inform me of what you learn?"

"I'll send FitzDuncan," Freddy said.

"Thank you, Lord Rawlinsford," Sir Oliver said.

Freddy rose and headed for the door. That signaled that the meeting was over, according to him. Sir Oliver handed me the piece of paper with Madam Traval's address. His eyes flicked towards Freddy, questioning. I shrugged my shoulders helplessly.

When we reached the street outside, Freddy asked, "How do you think that went?"

"Freddy, you were brilliant," I stated sincerely.

"I didn't come across as too snooty?"

"No. Your attitude was just right. By addressing him as a civil servant, which he is, you explained your presence and also prevented him from asking more probing questions. I don't know if you're aware, but it's not too unusual to see aristocrats insert themselves into matters about which they know nothing. I'm sure Sir Oliver faces that often."

"Well, I try not to do that," Freddy explained defensively. "But I've certainly seen it happen and was just trying to behave like that. I noticed you stayed away from our ideas about Albert being the actual target of what du Pais is planning."

"As I mentioned last night, Albert's involvement makes this much trickier," I said. "Whether we like him, he *is* the heir apparent. Sir Oliver is no fool. He will be able to make his own connection. Better for us to pretend ignorance than to appear to take a position. Did you notice that Sir Oliver did not answer your demand for information about the castle and our access?"

"Now that you mention it," Freddy commented.

"He absolutely does not want to provide either of those," I said. "To avoid denying you, he avoided answering. He will tell me 'no' when you send me to report on what we learn from Madam Traval. By then, it will be too late in the day for 'Lord Rawlinsford' to respond. That gives him more time to figure out how to handle the information he has."

"What do you mean?"

"The abduction of the girl is what set this off. She was taken from the street immediately after she had called upon me. She asked me earlier to find a way to get her out of the marriage. Because of that, Sir Oliver prevailed upon me to dig into this," I said.

"What do you get in return?" Freddy asked.

"Sir Oliver's good will," I snorted. "Considering that I occasionally encounter him while engaged in other business, having him in my debt should make my life easier. When he made the request, however, I don't think he thought it would involve Albert."

"It still might not," Freddy suggested. "Madam Traval may provide the answer to the whole matter. A ransom demand could appear."

"Let's hope."

The Traval home was in one of the nicest neighborhoods in the city. The houses were tall and substantial. Each one had a small yard in front, with most of them filled with flower gardens. Given that it was autumn, many of the gardens appeared lifeless. A few were filled with plants that thrive in this season. Traval's was dormant.

We climbed the steps to the front door. Before I rapped the knocker, Freddy stopped me. "You'll want this," he said.

He handed me a small card on heavy cream-colored paper. His name was engraved on it. I rapped with the knocker. A round-faced maid, quite homely, opened the door. Freddy stood, looking important and gazing down the street, while I spoke to her.

"Lord Rawlinsford here to call upon Madam Traval, miss," I uttered politely, handing her Freddy's card.

She bobbed politely in Freddy's direction, even though he wasn't paying her the slightest attention. "I'll see if she's receiving."

The door closed. I could hear the clack of her shoes on the floor. Freddy maintained his air of disinterest. I heard the maid approaching. The door opened.

"Won't you please come in," the maid said.

Freddy finally turned and deigned to notice her. He strode through the door as though he were entering his own house. He paused a few steps in, waiting for the maid to shut the door and lead him to Madam Traval. I tucked myself in behind Freddy and to his right, trying to be invisible like a good manservant should be. The girl led us down the hall to a parlor.

Madam Traval was there. Overweight, with unnaturally red hair that had to be dyed to be that color, and dressed in the latest fashion. It was not a becoming look on her. The tight bodice of the dress made her look like ten pounds of sausage in a five-pound casing. Her bosom was upthrust and constricted in a manner that looked painful. Her face was pretty, though. Her daughter had received some of her good looks from her mother. She attempted a small curtsy. Freddy gave her an insincere smile in response.

I took my station next to the door. I stood straight with my arms at my side. My job was to try to be a silent statue.

"Won't you please sit down, Lord Rawlinsford," she asked.

Freddy sat. He perched on the edge of the chair with his hands in his lap. His posture seemed to indicate the visit would be brief.

"May I offer you some refreshment?" she asked.

"Please," Freddy drawled.

Madam Traval took a small silver bell from the table next to her. She rang it. This amused me. Using a bell to beckon a servant was an affectation of the upper-middle class. They thought that was the refined method used to summon servants, believing that the upper class was at least that refined.

They would have been disappointed to learn the upper classes preferred to shout at the servants.

The homely maid entered, bearing a tea tray. She set it down on the table next to Madam Traval. She scurried out.

"Tea?" Madam Traval asked.

"Please."

She poured with shaking hands. One could hear the cup rattling in the saucer. She was aware of it, which made her even more nervous.

"Milk? Sugar?" she inquired.

"No, thank you," Freddy replied.

He leaned forward to take the cup before she spilled it. For her own cup, she wisely left it on the tray. She added two lumps of sugar. Freddy put his cup on the table next to him. He had not bothered to taste it.

"Biscuit?" she asked.

"No, thank you," he answered.

The tiniest look of disappointment clouded her expression. If her guest would not indulge, neither could she. I sensed she quite desired one of those biscuits.

"Madam," Freddy commenced, "I have been asked to see you regarding your daughter's disappearance. I apologize for mentioning a subject that I am sure is a great trial for you."

"It's very kind of you, milord," she replied. "It was a great concern for us."

"Was? It no longer troubles you?" he asked.

"The Viscount du Pais, her fiancé, called upon me yesterday and assured me we need not worry. He told me that a known criminal named Casimir FitzDuncan had taken her. That same man came to my husband's offices yesterday to present a ransom demand. Sadly, my husband did not know this at the time. He had his men throw this FitzDuncan out of the office instead of apprehending him."

"How much is this scoundrel demanding in ransom?" Freddy asked.

"The Viscount says he is demanding 500,000 ducats. The Viscount knows all about this FitzDuncan. He says FitzDuncan is an accomplished thief and blackmailer and always charges his victims half of an object's value to regain it. Since Julienne's dowry will be a million ducats, the Viscount believes FitzDuncan set her ransom at half that for her safe return."

"I see," Freddy responded. "And you are no longer troubled by this?"

"No," she answered confidently. "The Viscount knows where the villain is keeping her. He is gathering his retainers and plans to rescue Julienne tonight. The entire matter will be resolved in another day."

"I can see why you are no longer ill-at-ease about this, Madam," Freddy commented. "The Viscount is absolutely certain about this? The reason I ask... how can I put this delicately? There are rumors, Madam, that your daughter was… less than enthusiastic about the impending nuptials. Did she have another suitor? Or could her friends have helped organize her disappearance, trying to help her avoid a marriage about which she is uncertain?"

"The Viscount is entirely convinced regarding FitzDuncan being her kidnapper," she answered. "As far as other suitors, some families had inquired, but my husband had turned them all away. Regarding my daughter's feelings about marrying the Viscount, a bride-to-be is always nervous. I know I was. Yet, my marriage has turned out happily enough."

"Indeed," Freddy stated. "If I could, Madam, just to be able to wrap up any possible loose ends, I would like the names of your daughter's close friends. I would like to question them to make certain they were not involved with this FitzDuncan fellow."

"Oh, they are nice girls from good families," she stated. "I doubt they would have had anything to do with him."

Freddy gave her a patronizing smile. "Still, Madam, the folly of youth is such that — "

"Yes," she conceded. "You might be right. I would hate for them to be involved, but there's only one way to find out, I suppose."

"You can count on my discretion, of course," Freddy assured her.

Madam Traval rose and crossed to a desk in the corner of the room. She found a piece of paper and took a quill in hand. Laboriously, with the tip of her tongue sticking out the side of her mouth, she wrote something down. When she finished, she crossed back and handed it to Freddy. Freddy had already stood. He glanced briefly at the paper. Madam Traval's handwriting was childlike.

"If you would be so kind, Madam, as to have your girl show us out?"

Madam Traval rang her little bell. The homely maid appeared. After receiving her instructions, Freddy thanked Madam for her time. The maid then took us to the door. I followed Freddy, maintaining my position behind and to the right of him until we were out of sight of Traval's house.

"Majors and Minors, Caz!" Freddy exploded. "Do you believe that?!?"

"Whether or not I believe it, I have more immediate concerns," I replied, nodding past Freddy's shoulder.

I had seen the gleam of the breastplates and helmets of four members of the Castle Shield emerging from the market district of this part of town. The Shield was the name of the unit of elite troops stationed as guards to the royal family. Based on what Madam Traval had just shared, I suspected they were coming for me.

"Freddy, I need to run. Don't give them an excuse to drag you further into this, Freddy."

"This is so wrong, Caz," he muttered.

"Right and wrong don't matter to some, Freddy. You can interview the two friends if you think it will do any good," I suggested. "Though I think we can agree that's a dead end. Or you can storm into the Palace of Justice, even though Sir Oliver will say there is nothing he can do. Beyond that, I'm out of ideas. If they catch me, at least I figured out a way to get into the castle."

I took off at a jog and headed down the nearest side street. The soldiers saw me move and started to run. The longer I could make this chase, the better my chances were. They were wearing iron armor and helmets. That would get heavy quickly. My immediate goal was to reach the market. I hoped it would be crowded enough to enable me to slip away. Fortunately, my jacket and breeches were a dull buff color, nearly ideal for blending in.

Once I rounded the corner and was out of their sight, I picked up my pace to just short of an all-out sprint. I needed to pass the cross-street nearest to where they were before they reached the intersection. If I did, I liked my chances of reaching the market. If not, I might need to stand and fight.

My hope of making a clean escape evaporated when two of the soldiers emerged from the side street in front of me. The good news seemed to be that there were only two of them. The other two must have gone to talk to Freddy. The bad news is these were trained, experienced soldiers. I wouldn't be able to surprise them the way I had the thug.

I slowed to a walk, removing my jacket as I did. Grasping the collar in my left hand, I drew my sword with my right. When I had the jacket made, I sewed demi-florins, large copper coins, into the hem. If I could snap that weighted hem in the face of one, it might distract him enough to give me an opening. The weight in the hem also helped me wrap it around my left arm more quickly if I wanted to use it as a shield.

They were both right-handed. That helped me, too, if I moved quickly. It was also to my advantage that I did not need to subdue either of them. If I wounded them, I would run away.

"Casimir FitzDuncan?" called one.

"Aye."

"You're wanted by the Crown for questioning. Will you come peacefully?"

"If I had been asked by an unarmed messenger of the Crown, I'm sure I would have. Given that you're both soldiers, I think that is not in my best interest. Your appearance suggests it would be an unpleasant meeting."

He shrugged his shoulders. He didn't care. They approached carefully. They were far enough apart from one another that neither would get in the way of the other. I'd see if I could change that. I shuffled to my left quickly. Each of them rotated to face me. The one on the right, now behind his partner, took a half-step forward, drawing the two closer together. While they might be experienced soldiers, they weren't accustomed to fighting as a pair.

Before they had a chance to adjust their position, I yelled like a madman and whipped my jacket at the face of the one closest to me. I didn't connect, but he had leaned back. His thrust at me was chest-level because of his reaction. That worked well for me, as I was already dropping to my right knee. I drove my blade quickly into and out of his left thigh, then allowed my momentum to carry me, dropping my hip to the street and rolling over and up. His position had blocked his partner from being able to strike me. I shuffled backward to see what they would do.

The one had clapped his hand over his thigh. The second was distracted, looking at his wounded partner. Turning his attention back to me, he stepped forward to close within range. I yelled again, swinging my jacket. This time, I wasn't trying to smack his face. My jacket wrapped around my left forearm. He aimed for my gut. I blocked his strike with my protected left arm and stabbed him in the right thigh.

I didn't pause to assess the damage. I turned and ran. When I reached the edge of the market, I turned to look. The two of them were standing where I'd left them. Neither wound I'd dealt was serious. It was just enough to prevent them from continuing the chase. While the market was not packed with people, there were enough that I could weave between and around them and make it hard for the soldiers to follow my progress. I checked my jacket for damage. His weapon had sliced the lining, but the damage would not show once I had it on. I shrugged it onto my shoulders. Its dull color would make it even harder to spot me the deeper into the square I went.

Where to go? Not home. Not to Freddy's. The Palace of Justice? Perhaps. *Lucy's*, my mind suggested. *No-No-No-No*, I tried to tell myself. *Lucy's*, my mind repeated. The Palace of Justice, I decided.

I headed in that direction. I started at a fast walk, not wanting to draw attention by running. I was heading to the Palace of Justice. Why? Albert had ordered the men to come get me. Madam Traval told us that du Pais claimed I had made a request for ransom. Would Sir Oliver protect me? I didn't know whether he would. He would throw me in a cell and hold me until he investigated further. By then, the girl would likely be dead.

I once again found myself in the square where Lucy's shop was located. *Seven hells!* What happened? I'd been heading to the Palace of Justice. Her shop wasn't even on the way. My steps continued to pull me closer. I'd go to the back, at least.

When I reached the back door, I raised my hand to knock. The door opened before my hand struck. There stood Lucy.

"Hello, Caz," she said, smiling. "Your feet brought you here?"

"Um, Lady Darling, I'm not sure I should be here."

"If you continue to call me that, I'm not sure you're welcome," she teased. "What did I ask you to call me?"

"Lucy."

"You remembered, but you did not heed my wishes. How should I take that?"

"Arrghh!" I groaned. "Lucy, I apologize. I'm just very sensitive to who you are and who I am."

"We need to discuss that, but later," she said. "First, tell me why you shouldn't be here."

I did, letting her know I was now accused of kidnapping and on the run from the Castle Shield. "The last thing I want to do is expose you to suspicion or, worse, danger," I said in closing.

"Then why did you come?" she asked. If I had not been so distressed, I might have noticed the twinkle in her eye.

"Lucy, it's the strangest thing. I had determined that I would go to the Palace of Justice. While I was walking, I began thinking of my predicament and the next thing I knew; I was in this square. The same thing happened yesterday. I was not intending to come see you when suddenly, I was here. I don't understand it and can't explain it."

"Is it so bad, coming to see me?" she asked.

"I enjoy your company," I replied. "Perhaps more than I should. I'm sure my behavior is improper."

"It is," she scolded. I looked up, startled. "You kissed me on the cheek yesterday."

"Yes, milady. I'm sorry."

"I wanted you to kiss me on the lips," she complained.

Stunned, I stood agape. Lucy's musical laugh rang out. "Caz, sometimes you think too much," she said.

"Your brother said the same thing last night."

"Someday, perhaps, the message will make sense to you. So, the Castle Shield is looking for you. What about the Watch?"

"I don't know."

"I am sure they are."

"How?" I asked. Realizing that it wasn't important, I said urgently, "Then I should leave immediately."

"You will not," she stated forcefully. "Caz, though it might not seem like it, this is one of the safest places for you in all of Aquileia."

"How can you say that? Two members of the Shield stopped Freddy. If they took him in for questioning — "

"They didn't."

"Freddy came with me this morning to meet Sir Oliver — "

"Sir Oliver won't link that to me."

"How can you be so certain?" I asked.

"I just am," she answered. "You'll have to trust me, Caz. I know trust does not come easily to you, but try."

I hadn't noticed, but somewhere in our exchange, she clasped my hand. I turned to her. I looked into her pale blue eyes. "Lucy, I've only known you for two days, but if anything were to happen to you, I think it would destroy me. If it were because of me, I know it would."

I felt as though I had drawn a bucket from the deepest part of my emotional well. The bucket was full of tears, which were now threatening to flow down my cheeks. I had not felt emotions this strongly since the death of my grandfather. What was I doing? I had no business saying such things to a Lady. Yet, I could not deny that I felt so intensely.

Lucy stood on her tiptoes. She leaned forward. Her lips pressed to mine. "Trust me," she whispered.

When her lips brushed mine, my doubts, fears and insecurities disappeared like a land breeze dispelling fog.

"Better," she said. "So, what have you and Freddy been doing today?"

I told her about our visits to Sir Oliver and to Madam Traval. She asked about Freddy. I shared with her how brilliant Freddy had been in his 'Lord Rawlinsford' persona, both at the Palace of Justice and with Madam Traval.

"I must say, it's a side of Freddy I've never seen before," I admitted.

"Oh, that's not Freddy at all," she explained. "He was pretending to be someone else—probably a schoolmate. He's a gifted mimic."

"I don't remember that," I protested.

"You wouldn't. He would never have dared to display it at school or in front of the grown-ups. Majors and Minors, being an actor is even worse than owning a shop!"

I smiled and nodded, acknowledging her point.

"He would only trot it out in front of us, the cousins," she explained. "During the winter holidays, when the adults banished us to the upstairs so they could begin their drinking and gossip, Freddy would have us rolling on the floor, clutching our sides. He could imitate every one of the adults perfectly. Even better, he would have them say outrageous things that were even funnier because they fit each person so well. I particularly remember him as Grand-Nan, saying in her whiny voice that she would kill us all, except we were unworthy of her time and attention. Completely outrageous, yet somehow you knew it might not be far from the truth."

"Madam Traval sounds as though she is completely bewitched by Bergeron's title," Lucy continued. "Her family is quite wealthy. They married her to Traval because they liked his prospects. He used her dowry and made a fortune. As a girl, she was probably hoping to be matched with a member of the nobility and not another merchant. It would not surprise me to learn she was as much in favor of the match with Bergeron as her husband. She might even have been the instigator. She also provided Freddy with a tremendous excuse to explain away his involvement with you."

"How?" I asked.

"He'll adopt the same personality you saw with Sir Oliver. He'll initially defend you, as would be expected. When they make the claim that you're a kidnapper, blackmailer and a thief, and explain to Freddy that the reason you were able to get his ring back was because you were behind the whole affair, he will act as though he finally understands. His blustery display of his sense of betrayal will be something to see," she said with a giggle. "Because they will think he's stupid enough to have believed them, they might let something slip in front of him that will help us."

"How did you know about the ring?" I asked. "I thought Freddy would take that secret to the grave with him."

"Hmmm," she replied. "I meant to ask you; what sort of surprise did Theo leave for you last night?"

"None. And he didn't try to poison my breakfast this morning either."

"That's incredible! How did you do that?"

"I threatened him with bodily harm. After leaving you yesterday, I was waylaid in the street. By the time I reached Freddy's, I was in no mood to tolerate Theo's little jokes. I did tell him, after breakfast, that when this matter is all wrapped up in a couple of days, he can return to tormenting me to his heart's content."

"That was sweet of you," Lucy said.

# 6

Poor Freddy. When I deserted him in the street, I left him in a situation he never experienced before. He would be the first to admit (and did, later) that he had led a sheltered and dull life. It was why he was so enthusiastic about helping me. Having two members of the Castle Shield run up to him with swords drawn was, perhaps, more excitement than he wanted. He quickly adopted the persona I'd seen earlier, which I called his 'Lord Rawlinsford' character (it was actually his imitation of a former schoolmate—when he told me who it was, I laughed at his accuracy).

"Are you Casimir FitzDuncan?" one of the soldiers asked.

"Good gods, no, man!" he exclaimed. "Don't you know who I am?"

The soldier shook his head. Freddy gave an exasperated sigh. "I'm Lord Rawlinsford, you dolt. What's this all about?"

"Was the man with you Casimir FitzDuncan?"

"Yes. What of it?"

"He is to be arrested for kidnapping," the soldier explained. "And we are to bring you to the castle."

"Preposterous!" Freddy retorted. "FitzDuncan is no more a kidnapper than I am. And I'm not some common criminal you can drag off. If I'm to go to the castle, I'll respond to a proper invitation."

The second soldier recognized the type of person 'Lord Rawlinsford' was, and tried a different approach. "Milord, we apologize for any misunderstanding. As you can imagine, this is a matter of great urgency. You would be of great assistance to the Crown if you would be so kind as to go to the castle and answer some questions. Your knowledge will be of the utmost help and may be crucial to our understanding."

Impressed by the soldier's smarminess, Freddy pretended to be appeased. "That's a different proposition, then. Very well, you may tell them I will call on them this afternoon."

"Won't you come with us?" asked the first soldier.

"Majors and Minors, no, man! I have plans for lunch at my club. I will come answer your questions afterward."

"That would be most helpful of you, milord," the second soldier responded. "Thank you."

"Hmmph!" Freddy snorted. "We are finished here. Good day," he said, as he started to walk away.

He left the two soldiers behind as he strolled away. His casual confidence left them speechless. Inside, Freddy was shaking. He headed in the direction of his club in case the soldiers thought to check up on him. Thinking better of walking, he hailed a hackney when he arrived at the market square.

"Is your shop closed?" I asked. "I don't want to keep you from your customers."

"Don't worry about that," she replied. "They'll come when I'm ready for them. What is the next step for you, as far as rescuing Miss Traval?"

"I'm stymied right now," I said. "With the Castle Shield and City Watch both looking for me, there's not much I can do."

"What would you do if you could?"

"I'd like to find Miss Traval before tonight."

"Why?"

"If I can find her before tonight, perhaps I can save her."

"Where do you think she is?"

"The du Pais estate is less than ten leagues away. I am guessing he took her there and is having his people keep watch over her. It's the most secure place, but I could be wrong. He could have her anywhere in the city."

"And if you can't find her? What then?"

"Then I need to figure out a way into the castle," I said. "Once I'm in the castle, I need to find the room where du Pais has his little ceremony planned. I suppose then, I burst in, shout 'Aha!' and stop the proceedings. That is complicated, though. It would be easier if I found her before."

"If you find her before, would you return her to her parents, who will force her to marry Bergeron?"

"I'd prefer not to," I admitted.

"Then, in the eyes of the law and of her father, you would indeed be a kidnapper," Lucy explained. "Mr. Traval is very rich. He could hire people to chase you to the ends of the earth. Is that what you want?"

"No," I responded. "But it's less complicated."

"Which complication worries you the most?" she asked.

Damme! This woman had a way of drawing out of me the things I didn't want to share.

"What troubles me the most, Lucy, is the prospect of bursting into the room and catching Albert in the middle of this hideous thing," I admitted.

"I don't like Albert. I think his character is weak. From what I've seen, his younger brother would make a much better ruler. But to put myself in as the fulcrum on which these events hinge—that's not my place."

"Because you're a bastard?"

"No. Because I'm not the king. Nor do I claim to know either of them well enough to make such a decision."

"What if the king were present for your 'aha' moment?" she asked.

"Do you understand how impossible this is?" I protested. "I have to get into the castle—something that won't happen. Then, figure out where in that immense building to go without drawing attention. Now you suggest I invite the king to come watch? If I tried to see him, they would cut me down. Impossible, improbable and impossible. Furthermore, your shop seems to be the only place in the city where I won't be arrested."

"You already know how to get in the castle," she suggested.

"What?" I objected.

"Sure. Walk up to one of the Castle Shield who is looking for you and turn yourself in," she teased.

"That gets me into the castle—in a cell, below ground, likely never to see the light of day again," I commented sarcastically.

"Well, think about it," she said. "Go upstairs and keep Chauncey company. There are some customers who are coming. When I've finished with them, I'll come up and we can get something to eat."

I headed up the stairs to her sitting room. Chauncey the owl opened his eyes when I entered. He fluffed himself, then settled and closed his eyes again. I sat in the same chair as before, near his perch.

One thing my grandfather taught me is to break big problems into smaller pieces. I faced a big problem and couldn't find any solutions. I tried to divide what I was facing into smaller pieces. I didn't have much success.

Albert was the complication. If this were just a case of kidnapping, I would have started in a different direction, focusing on finding the girl and freeing her. Albert, the apparently willing victim, complicated everything. It brought the weight of the Crown and the government into it. It was a matter of state, not just a criminal act.

Where to go and what to do? I wondered. Despite what I'd said earlier, I decided I wasn't exactly trapped in Lucy's shop. Though the Castle Shield and City Watch were looking for me, only a few members of the Watch might know me on sight. I simply needed to stay away from places where I was known. That meant my rooms and the area nearby them, Freddy's house and the more exclusive clubs in the city.

Something had changed between this morning when Freddy and I had called upon Sir Oliver and now. Madam Traval had said the Viscount claimed I had made my ransom demand yesterday. We'd met with Sir Oliver earlier and he had said he knew of no demand. That meant that 'my' demand for ransom had just been communicated. The involvement of the Castle Shield indicated that a member of the Royal family was interceding. To my mind, that meant Albert. If somehow I could gain a meeting with Wim, I hoped I could explain things and get him to help me thwart this scheme of the Viscount.

I certainly could not approach Wim, but Freddy could. Of course, I had no idea where Freddy was or if he had been taken into custody. If he were still at large, he would be either at home with Theo or at the Equestrian Club. My guess was the club.

I heard Lucy coming up the stairs, humming a pleasant tune. "Have you and Chauncey figured everything out?" she asked.

"Not yet," I responded. "But I have an idea."

"Good. You can tell me about it over lunch," she replied. "We're going to a café around the corner."

I followed her down the stairs and out the back door into the alley. I offered her my arm, and she grasped the inside of my right elbow with her left hand. It was the normal polite gesture, something I'd done for dozens of women before. With Lucy, it felt more important than that, somehow.

When we had been seated and served, I shared with her my idea to plead my case to Wim somehow. She agreed it seemed like a good idea. She also agreed that Freddy would be the best person to arrange it.

"We can have a boy take a message to him at the Equestrian Club," she said.

"How do you know he's there?" I asked.

"He always goes there," she replied. "It's his home away from home."

Before I could ask the next question, she answered it. "There are a couple of boys in the neighborhood who love to run errands for me because I reward them with sweets. Where should we have Freddy meet you? At the shop?"

"I've imposed upon your good nature enough, Lucy," I responded. "There's an inn named the 'Foaming Boar' where I will go. The owner is a trusted friend. I'll take a room there."

Though the best idea I had was to ask Wim for his assistance, I didn't want to involve Wim any further than I needed to. Pierre Luin's description of trying to juggle a ball of tar came to mind. I was beginning to feel that I was the ball of tar.

After lunch, I walked Lucy back to her shop. She said she would have a boy deliver a message to Freddy. I took my leave. I walked around to the front of the building to the square. There was a hackney waiting, the horse nosing halfheartedly in a feed bag. The driver had his hat tilted down and appeared to be napping. I walked up to him.

"Would you like a fare?"

He snapped awake. "By all means, sur. Where to, sur?"

"The Foaming Boar. It's an inn. Know it?"

"Yes, sur."

He slid down and opened the hackney for me. I climbed in. Within a short time, we were moving. The slight delay was, I imagined, his retrieving the feed bag. When we reached the Foaming Boar, he opened the door for me.

"Four florins, sur," he said.

I gave him a five-florin piece and nodded that he should keep it.

"Thankee, sur."

I waited for him to drive off. When he was out of sight, I went around to the rear of the inn. I entered through the kitchen, getting some strange looks from the cooks. I found Carl Stensland behind the bar. I tucked myself up against the wall and cleared my throat to get his attention.

He looked my way and raised an eyebrow at my somewhat hidden position. He looked out over the room and saw no one was looking his way. "How can I help you, Cap'n?"

"Sar'nt, right now the City Watch and the Castle Shield are both looking for me for something I didn't do. I was hoping I could rent one of your rooms until I can straighten this out. If that makes you uncomfortable, tell me and I'll be on my way."

"What do they want you for?" he asked.

"Kidnapping, thievery, blackmail… the usual," I answered cheekily.

He tilted his head, then grinned. "I didn't know you had it in you, Cap'n. Good for you. Go on up the back stairs. I'll meet you."

I retraced my steps through the kitchen to the back stairway. I met him at the other end of the hallway. He handed me a key.

"#3," he said. "As long as you need it. Anything else?"

"A gent might come calling for me. Tall, thin, light brown hair. Name is Lord Rawlinsford. Please send him up."

The room was small, simple and plain. There was a bed, a chair and a small table with a lamp. In the drawer of the table were some matches. The walls were white. There were no pictures hanging on them. The floor was bare.

I stretched out on the bed to wait for Freddy. The pleasant lunch I'd enjoyed with Lucy weighed my eyelids down. I dozed lightly. A soft knock on the door woke me. I scrambled up and opened it to see Freddy.

"It's good to see you," I told him sincerely.

"You're a kidnapper, you know," he replied.

"Not to mention a thief and a blackmailer," I replied.

Freddy explained what happened to him after I ran away. He recounted how he had put the soldiers on their back feet with his arrogance. He told me he was on his way to the castle to answer their summons but stopped to see me first, having received the note from Lucy.

"Freddy, I don't know if it will be possible, but if you can, I'd like to arrange a meeting with Wim. I think if I can tell him the whole story, he can help put me in the clear."

"I'll do what I can," Freddy promised.

"Now, Freddy, when you get to the castle, you'll probably be directed to Albert. He will probably present the same things we heard from Madam Traval. Do not defend me. Listen to what he says and pretend to believe him. Act outraged at my deception."

"But Caz, it's all so preposterous," he protested.

"Don't think that way," I urged. "Think instead that what they tell you is reasonable and sane. Work yourself into righteous indignation over my lies and betrayal."

"Why? Why should I?" he asked.

"Because there's a possibility I might not be able to clear my name," I answered. "Bergeron seems to be one step ahead of me. If this ends badly, I don't want your reputation to suffer from our association."

"This whole situation is beginning to anger me," Freddy said tensely. "You and I are trying to do the right thing, but everyone and everything seems to be working against us. Just now, at the club, no one would speak to me. They shunned me as though I had a disease."

"It does seem our opponents have the better cards this hand," I admitted. "As far as the reaction of others, I apologize. For now, go to the castle. Put up with Albert and try to catch Wim's attention before you leave."

"Right," Freddy confirmed, then left.

Freddy took a hackney to the castle gate. He went to the guard house. He addressed the man on duty.

"Lord Rawlinsford," he drawled. "Here by invitation of the Crown."

"Yes, milord," the guard responded. "If you'll excuse me, I'll send word that you've arrived."

The guard had no idea who Lord Rawlinsford was or if he'd been invited to the castle. He ordered one of the pages to run to the castle with the information. Someone there would make the decision about what to do with Lord Rawlinsford.

The guard returned to his post. "I apologize, milord," he explained. "I just sent a message across that you were here. They had not warned me to expect you. I expect someone will be here presently to escort you. I'm sorry about the delay."

Freddy harumphed in response. He waited, pretending annoyance. He told me later that enough time passed that he was beginning to consider leaving in an arrogant huff. Just then, a boy appeared.

The boy was red in the face from running. He was trying to control his breathing. He looked and saw Freddy.

"Milord," the boy said with a bow. "If you would please come with me."

The page led Freddy to one of the smaller reception chambers in the castle. Waiting there was Albert. Bergeron du Pais was sitting next to him. There was an empty chair in front of them.

The page announced him: "Lord Rawlinsford to see His Highness."

Albert waved the boy off. He stood. "Thank you for coming, Lord Rawlinsford," he said in an oily voice. "Please sit."

"What's this all about, Your Highness? It was most upsetting to be accosted on the street by members of the Castle Shield."

"I apologize for that," Albert replied in a tone that conveyed he felt no remorse at all. "We are in the midst of an urgent situation. The pressing nature of the matter took precedence over normal discretion. Your friend FitzDuncan is at the heart of it, I'm afraid."

"I wouldn't go so far as to call him a friend," Freddy sniffed. "Merely an acquaintance who did me a favor at one time."

"About that favor," du Pais interjected. "That would be when he helped you regain a ring you had offered as surety in a game of cards with Sir Edmund Tourville?"

"Yes," Freddy replied. "How did you learn of this?" he asked in an indignant tone, clearly annoyed that someone else knew of it.

"Would it interest you to know that Sir Edmund was an accomplice of FitzDuncan's?" du Pais added.

"Preposterous!" Freddy exclaimed. "FitzDuncan helped me get the ring back from that scoundrel."

"Easily done since Sir Edmund took the ring from you upon instructions from FitzDuncan," du Pais said calmly. "It worked out even better for FitzDuncan when you approached him to enlist his aid in getting it back. Tell me, did FitzDuncan approach you and offer his assistance?"

"I don't rightly recall," Freddy answered, though he remembered clearly that he had approached me.

"It's not really important," du Pais admitted. "But it worked out better for FitzDuncan than he originally planned. He was blackmailing Sir Edmund and forced him to obtain the ring from you. FitzDuncan was planning to blackmail you, using the ring as leverage. He has been following the same pattern since he was drummed out of the Rangers."

"He told me he'd left the Rangers," Freddy countered.

"Of course he did," Albert said. "No one would ever want to admit they were cashiered."

"Regardless, FitzDuncan used your awkward situation to his advantage," du Pais explained. "Not only did he benefit financially in greater measure than he had hoped, but the victim of the crime was completely unaware of his involvement. In fact, he used you to spread word of his trustworthiness to other victims of his, like Pierre Luin and Sir John Dunleavy. I'm sure you will be chagrined to realize that your recommendation helped him make Luin and Sir John willing victims who helped him expand his reach further. We estimate that he now has fleeced well over a dozen people in this way."

"How did you learn of this?" Freddy asked, pretending to be shocked and dismayed while still portraying a sense of disbelief.

"Sir Edmund Tourville," du Pais replied. "FitzDuncan did substantial damage to his reputation. Sir Edmund was overheard to complain about it after having too much to drink one night. It came to the Crown's attention. When pressed, Sir Edmund admitted the whole thing. With that information, we also questioned Luin and Sir John."

"Majors and Minors!" Freddy exclaimed. "I feel such a fool!"

"You're not the only one," Albert said reassuringly. "Now, the reason you are here. FitzDuncan has kidnapped a young lady, Miss Julienne Traval. Miss Traval is engaged to marry the Viscount. Her father has generously offered a dowry of a million ducats. FitzDuncan has threatened to kill the young lady unless he is paid half that amount."

Freddy gave them a look of confusion.

"Something troubles you, Lord Rawlinsford?" du Pais asked.

"Yes, Viscount. You see, FitzDuncan claims you are the likely kidnapper."

"As we know," Albert stated, smiling smugly. "Tell me. What sort of man needs to kidnap his own bride-to-be?"

"Well, he told a story of the marriage contract, which would pay Bergeron here, regardless of whether the marriage took place. He claimed that Sir Oliver West had begged him to look into the matter."

"I assure you, Lord Rawlinsford, I would prefer to have the girl," du Pais stated.

"Sir Oliver acted upon our instructions," Albert added. "But he did not beg FitzDuncan to look into this matter. Quite the contrary, he informed FitzDuncan that we were aware of his scheme and would not allow him to get away with it."

"I'm so embarrassed," Freddy muttered.

"You can help us," Albert offered.

"How?"

"FitzDuncan has threatened to kill the young lady if his demands are not met by tonight. We have sent soldiers and the City Watch to arrest him. We will question him as harshly as necessary to learn where he is keeping the girl," Albert explained. "It would be helpful to us if you could arrange a meeting with him this evening. Set the meeting for a place where we could have men waiting."

"I don't know where he is," Freddy admitted. "He has been staying at my place the last two nights, claiming he fears that you, Viscount, will send someone to burn his building to the ground. He knows you are looking to apprehend him, so I don't believe he will stay with me this evening."

"Tell him you have arranged a meeting with my brother," Albert suggested. "Wim always did a better job of pretending not to despise the man than I did. Perhaps he thinks Wim can help him escape the noose that is surely waiting for him."

"He did mention that he wanted to speak with Wim," Freddy admitted. "Though he didn't tell me why. Where and when should I tell him the meeting is?"

"Later this afternoon," Albert replied. "At your house. Say—five o'clock. That will give our people an opportunity to find him and bring him in without your involvement, but if they can't, we can arrest him as he approaches your house."

7

With time running out, I decided I could no longer put off calling on Sir Oliver again. He had dumped this mess on me and I needed his help to resolve it. I had a nagging feeling he had not told me everything I needed to know.

I needed him to get me into the castle. He could tell me where in the castle it was likely du Pais would stage his dreadful ceremony. He might also be willing to give me assistance of some sort, though I wasn't counting on that.

Lucy had said that the City Watch was also hunting for me. How she knew that I didn't understand. She told me to trust her, so I did.

I decided the bold approach was the best. A hackney took me and dropped me off at the administrative entrance. I marched in the entrance hall and past the scribe waiting at the end.

"Sir Oliver is expecting me," I said as I walked by. "I'm late."

I was through the door before he had a chance to object. In a snap, I clambered up the stairs. Giving no one the opportunity to question or stop me, I strode down the hall and into his office, shutting the door behind me.

"Hello, Ollie," I said.

"Seven hells!" he exclaimed. "How did you get in here?"

"I marched right in," I said as I sat. "Rather quickly and boldly, if I do say so."

"My people are looking for you right now," he stated.

"I know. Why?"

"Orders from the Crown," he replied. "Same as before. They passed along your demand for 500,000 ducats to ransom the girl."

"Ollie, when you forced me into this, you said you knew I didn't kidnap the girl. Now? I'm the prime suspect?"

"An accusation like this must be investigated," he answered lamely. "I need to arrest you and hold you until we can make inquiries."

"You already know I didn't do it!" I almost shouted.

"New information has been given to me, which I must look into," he replied.

I shared with him the key point I had omitted that morning—that the planned ceremony was not aimed at giving du Pais magical powers but giving him control over Albert. Albert's participation in the proceedings, willing or not, would compromise him. The Viscount would have Albert under his control. The girl would die.

"And it looks as though they are trying to pin this on me," I concluded. "Your lack of involvement is an indication to me you don't object to that. I'm being accused of thievery, blackmail and kidnapping — "

"And murder," Sir Oliver added. "Algernon Toohey's body was found this morning. His throat was cut ear-to-ear."

"Who is Algernon Toohey?" I asked.

"You claim you smashed his face in," Sir Oliver answered.

"I told you so," I said. "I told you when you informed me of his release that he'd turn up dead."

"That certainly doesn't absolve you, FitzDuncan," he snapped. "It makes you an even more likely suspect."

"Because I predicted that whoever hired him to attack me would kill him to keep his mouth shut?"

"Because you killed him to keep his mouth shut after he staged an attack on you to divert suspicion away from yourself."

I sat there for a moment, stunned that Sir Oliver would say this. "Do you realize how improbable that sounds?" I asked.

"Whoever hired him never met Toohey," Sir Oliver explained. "Toohey was a low-level member of a gang. The person hiring him would have dealt with the gang leader, who then assigned the job to Toohey. Therefore, it's equally improbable that whoever hired him would need to kill him. Toohey had no more idea who was behind it than the man in the moon."

"What do you think, Sir Oliver?" I demanded. "I've shared with you everything I've learned. Well, everything except our interview with Madam Traval, which took place after we left this morning. The Viscount has informed her I am responsible for her daughter's kidnapping, but it will all be resolved by tomorrow. Do you believe du Pais, Sir Oliver? If it is to be resolved by tomorrow, I know how it will end for the girl. Or do you believe me?"

"He has witnesses prepared to testify against you," Sir Oliver said emphatically. "You have supposition and guesses."

"Witnesses? To what?" I demanded.

"Witnesses who will swear you are a thief, a blackmailer and now a murderer."

"They're lying," I stated.

"He also has the support of the Crown."

"If it's Albert, disregard it," I countered. "Albert is proving to be the most willing victim I've ever heard of. He's actually helping du Pais tie the noose around his own neck. You're the one who compelled me to look into this. Shouldn't that, at least, give me some credibility? If you can hold off arresting me for a few more hours and can get us into the castle, I'll be able to prove that what I've said is true."

"What will you show me?"

"If there is a place in the castle that would have some religious association, that's where du Pais will stage this. Is there something like that?" I asked.

"Yes," Sir Oliver replied with a sigh. "There's a shrine to Fortuna on the lower level. The first of the Gau kings built it to commemorate his victory and winning the throne."

"Anything else like that?"

"No. That's the only one I know," Sir Oliver replied.

"Then tonight, du Pais will stage a black wedding in that shrine," I responded. "Let me explain again. It's a wedding ceremony where all prayers are offered to the Lord of the Seven Hells. Then they will rape the bride. After that, they will slit her throat. The ritual is one that binds the officiant to the Lord of the Seven Hells and awakens his or her power in the dark arts. Bergeron knows he has no magical ability. While the ceremony would certainly bind him to evil, he won't gain any magical power from it. He's probably convinced Albert and others that they will gain magical powers by participating along with him. They won't. If Albert takes part, Bergeron will use that. He will threaten to expose Albert's involvement. It would prevent Albert from assuming the throne or from keeping the throne once he ascends. That is Bergeron's goal in this."

Sir Oliver sighed. "What do you want me to do?"

"Come with me," I replied. "Get us into the castle. The ceremony will be timed to conclude with her death at midnight because the second new moon of the month overlaps—the second new moon of a month and midnight have some meaning with the dark arts."

"How do you know this?" he asked.

"Someone familiar with the so-called ritual of awakening told me this. I'm not going to share the name. You need to get us into the shrine to Fortuna so we can prevent the ritual from taking place. Are you willing to do that?"

I sat back and folded my arms across my chest. Sir Oliver was wrestling with his thoughts. I waited for him to reach a conclusion.

"Fine," he breathed heavily. "Meet me at 9 o'clock, at the corner of Front and Bassett. I'll get you into the castle."

"One last thing. How do I get out of here without getting arrested?"

He gave a sad chuckle. "I'll walk you out to where you can hire a cab," he offered.

We left his office. He accompanied me to the area in front of the main entrance where there were cabs waiting. I took one, giving the driver my usual address at the bookseller. Once we were away, I opened the small window in the hackney and gave him a new destination, about a block away from the Foaming Boar.

Going through the rear entrance of the inn, I went up to my room. I didn't trust Sir Oliver. The Crown was putting pressure on him. They claimed to have witnesses who would swear to crimes I supposedly committed. That's a powerful argument for the Principal of the City Watch. There were no other choices available.

I was hoping Freddy had better results than I did. If he could speak with Wim and arrange a meeting, it might eliminate my need to rely on Sir Oliver. Considering that I had the feeling Sir Oliver would betray me, it was definitely the better option.

It wasn't long before Freddy knocked on the door of the room. He entered, looking pale. I could tell his meeting had not been successful.

"You look worried," I commented.

"I *am* worried," he replied. "Caz, they claim they can produce witnesses who will swear that you were an accomplice in the theft of my ring, in the theft of the letters you retrieved for Pierre Luin, and in whatever you did for Sir John Dunleavy. The story they tell is plausible."

"How do they explain that you approached me to help regain your ring?" I asked.

"They say it was a happy accident," Freddy responded. "They say that you changed your strategy when I asked for your help. They claim you saw an opportunity to get nearly as much money by pretending to help me and then use me to help convince other victims of yours to enlist your services. By pretending to help, it lowered your risk dramatically and ensured that no one would complain about what you had done."

"Did they convince you?" I asked.

"To believe them, I'd have to be as simple-minded as they think I am. I know what happened," Freddy stated confidently. "It puts you in an unpleasant situation, though. If you were brought to trial, in order to defend yourself in court, you would need to ask the people you've helped, like me, to come forward. I'm probably the only one who wouldn't be concerned. I already confessed to my father what happened. He chastised me for being an idiot and told me how lucky I was to have had your help. I would have no problem testifying in court on your behalf."

"Were you able to see Wim?" I asked.

"No," he replied. "They suggested I tell you I have arranged a meeting at my house this afternoon at five o'clock. They plan to apprehend you there."

"Thank you, Freddy. I'll be sure to stay away. I am to meet Sir Oliver at nine o'clock near the gate," I informed him. "He promised he would accompany me into the castle. Apparently, there is a shrine to Fortuna on the lower level. That's where I suspect the ceremony will be."

"Do you have any other ideas?" Freddy asked.

"Only one, and I give it an extremely low chance of success," I said.

"What?"

"I take a horse, wait out on the north road for the du Pais carriage, stop it and rescue the girl," I explained. "Like a highwayman. If they're accusing me of all these other crimes, I might as well act like a criminal."

"Are you sure they took her to the du Pais estate? They haven't hidden the girl in the city?" Freddy asked.

"I have no idea where they've hidden her," I confessed. "She could already be in the castle, for all I know. I tend to doubt that, however. Hiding her in the castle is too daring, too bold. There are too many eyes that could see. Albert doesn't strike me as that willing to take a risk. There are plenty of places they could have kept her in the city, though."

"If you don't believe they took her out of the city, then why wait on the road?"

"Because I want to do something," I responded angrily. "I feel like I've been jerked around like a puppet and I don't like it. I know a suitable spot on the north road. I should be able to catch them unawares."

"You'll need help," Freddy stated.

"No, Freddy," I responded quickly. "Absolutely not. Your reputation is already tarnished because of our association."

"Caz, there will be at least three of them," he pointed out.

"Freddy, you have a fighter's spirit, I'll grant you. What you lack is practical experience. I'd be more worried about keeping you safe than the girl," I explained.

"What about someone else?" Freddy asked. "You said the owner of this inn was a Ranger."

"Damme, Freddy, but that's a good idea," I exclaimed. "Please. Go see if the innkeeper can spare a minute to come chat."

Freddy bolted out of the room. He returned minutes later with Carl in tow. Carl stepped into the room.

"What can I do for you, Cap'n?"

"Sar'nt, can you assemble three men, armed, with horses, who can ride out on the north road with me in the next hour? I'll need a mount, too," I asked.

Stensland scratched his head. "What's the plan, Cap'n?"

"There might be a carriage coming into the city on the north road," I explained. "Inside the carriage will be a girl who was kidnapped a few days ago. I'd like to rescue the girl."

"Pardon my asking, Cap'n, but isn't this something for the City Watch?" he asked.

"So far, the City Watch doesn't seem to be interested in finding this girl, let alone freeing her. They think I kidnapped her. If anyone will rescue her, it will be me, or us," I said. "There's no guarantee that there will be a carriage. They might have hidden her somewhere in the city."

"What are you offering?" Stensland asked.

"Five ducats apiece?" I suggested. "Plus, a ducat to borrow a good horse for a few hours and likely get him some good exercise?"

Carl scratched his head. "A ducat for the horse is about right," he said. "Don't offer the men more than three ducats. Seven hells, they'd do it for free, just to get out of the house and have some excitement. I'd like to join you myself. Sure, I'll have your three men for you."

"And a horse?"

"Mine," he replied. "Stabled out back. He's a good 'un. Decent speed and stamina. Could use a good run outside of the city. Bring him back in one piece, Cap'n. I'll add the charge to your bill. The men will be here by four o'clock."

With that, he left.

"Freddy, that was a brilliant idea," I admitted. "As I said, there's no certainty that there will be a carriage. Even if there is, there's no telling if we'll be able to stop them. If either of those is the case, I intend to keep my appointment with Sir Oliver at nine o'clock."

"Is there anything I can do?" he pleaded.

"Freddy, you've done everything anyone could have hoped," I said humbly. "Whatever debt you felt you owed me has been more than repaid. I am extremely grateful for your assistance."

"Caz, it has been the most fun I've had in ages," Freddy replied. "I wouldn't mind helping you in the future if you need me. I hope you do. I'll go tell Albert and Bergeron that I wasn't able to find you to arrange the meeting."

He departed. I was left on my own. I tried to work through different possibilities in my head.

Sir Oliver West had compelled me to pursue this investigation. I'd taken two knocks on the head, been threatened two other times, been thrown out of an office, been accused of being a criminal and was subject to arrest. On top of that, I doubted whether I could count on Sir Oliver.

The only good thing to come from this whole affair was meeting Lucy, Lady Darling. Fat lot of good that did me. A bastard like me had no hope of winning the heart or the hand of a woman like her. Still, the time I had spent in her company had been the bright spot.

I headed down the back stairs and crossed to the stable. Carl had already asked a boy to ready the horse. The boy handed me the reins, telling me the horse's name, Andy. I checked the girth. The boy had done a good job.

"I should be back in a few hours," I said. I flipped him a half-florin. He snagged it out of the air, looked at it, and grinned.

"Thankee, sur," he said.

I stepped into the stirrup and hoisted myself into the saddle. It had been weeks since I'd sat a horse. I knew I'd feel it later. I walked Andy around the small yard. He was well-trained and not irritable at all. The three men showed up shortly after. Two of them, Robby and Bert, I knew from the Rangers. The other, Hank, was also a former Ranger but served on a different section of the border. Robby and Bert knew him, though. I explained to the men what I hoped to do.

"We'll ride out the north gate. There's a swale about a league out. We'll wait there. We're looking for a carriage with the du Pais coat of arms. I'll recognize it if it comes. There will be a girl inside. We want to stop the carriage and rescue the girl. That's if there's a carriage at all. We might just be riding out to sit in wait for no good reason. Any questions?"

"How many?" Hank asked.

I shook my head. "I don't know," I answered. "I'm guessing three. There could be more. Could be outriders. I don't have any information. I'm sorry."

"Carl's note said there's three ducats in it for each of us," Robby stated. "No offense, Cap'n, but — "

I smiled. "No offense taken, Robby."

I reached into my money pouch. Digging with my fingers, I retrieved three ducats for each of them in smaller change. Robby's concern was valid. If I fell, they wouldn't get paid. That nearly emptied my pouch.

It was just nearing five o'clock now. Albert and Bergeron would be approaching Freddy's house with their men. I was certain that both men would treat Freddy poorly since he didn't bring me into their trap.

We set off for the north gate of the city. It took us longer than thirty minutes to get there. Once past the gate, we were on open road. With the day ending, the traffic was all headed into the city, not in our direction. Traffic grew thinner the further we went. No one wanted to be in the open after dark.

We found the swale I remembered. We drew off the road. The swale curled around. Within a matter of a few yards, we were able to tuck ourselves around the curve, out of sight from the road. I dismounted and climbed the shallow slope where I could see the road. When I was halfway up, I reminded the men the waiting was the worst part, and there might not be a carriage at all.

I lay on my stomach, watching the road. The sun was on the horizon. Shadows were as long as they were going to get. From here, the light would fade. The men were chatting quietly among themselves.

More time passed. The light grew dim, and the air grew chill. I guessed we had been there for more than an hour. In another twenty minutes, we wouldn't be able to see anything and would need to wait next to the road and depend on our ears.

Just as I was about to give up, I saw a four-horse coach approaching. I peered through the growing darkness. I watched. What I saw was disappointing.

There was a coat of arms on the door of the coach. I couldn't make it out, but it didn't matter. There were two men on top of it and four others mounted, riding alongside—two in front and two at the rear. I scrambled quietly down the slope.

"Bad news, men," I announced. "The carriage we've been waiting for is coming, but there are two men on top and four outriders. That's too many."

The three put their heads together and mumbled softly. I couldn't hear what they were saying. I lifted myself into the saddle.

"Ah, Cap'n," Bert said. "If it's all the same to you, we'd like to give it a go."

I looked at them. Even in the growing gloom, I could tell all three were smiling. I could see their teeth in the fading light.

"It'll be fun, Cap'n," Hank said.

"Fine," I said. "Let's edge up to the road. We'll wait for them and try to head off the two lead riders. If we can whittle down the numbers, we can try to take the coach."

We waited. The carriage and riders were traveling at an easy trot. That made it easier to intercept them but also meant their horses had plenty of wind.

We heard them before we could see them. They came into view shortly after. We waited. The horse of the nearest outrider smelled us and whinnied.

"Go!" I said, putting spurs to Andy.

We leapt out of the darkness, but the outrider's horse had warned them about something. We did not take them completely by surprise. I rode at the first rider on the far side, my sword drawn. He was ready for me. We met and steel clanged on steel. The trailing rider on this side came up, and I was now trying to fight both of them.

Andy responded to the nudge of my knee and twirled away from them. I heard the snap of a whip as the drivers urged the carriage horses to run. I could hear the sounds of the fight on the other side, including the squeal of a frightened horse and a loud curse shouted into the night. The two riders I was fighting wheeled quickly around to attack me. The carriage pulled away swiftly.

Almost all my attention was centered on the two in front of me. I was able to prevent them from injuring me but was unable to deal a wounding blow in return. I freely admit that Andy may have saved my life. He side-hopped, unbidden. A slash I couldn't parry missed me entirely. It would have carved my shoulder in two if it hadn't been for Andy.

I heard a whistle. Suddenly, my two opponents broke off and galloped after the carriage. The two riders in the other tangle did the same. I noticed only two of my companions were mounted. I drew closer and saw that Bert was not with them. He trotted up on foot a moment later.

"Sorry, Cap'n," he said, panting. "The blackguard slashed at Simba's eyes. She's not a Ranger horse, sur. She reared and bolted. Dragged me a fair piece, she did."

"How about you?" I asked the others.

"Just a scratch," Hank replied.

I could see him clutching his upper left arm. Blood covered his hand and had soaked his sleeve. I nudged Andy closer to him. I grasped my knife and cut the seam at the top of the sleeve.

"Let go of your arm," I told him.

I tore the sleeve away and used it to bind his arm where I thought the wound was. I tied the ends around, trying to make it snug but not too tight. Some pressure would slow the bleeding. Too much pressure might cost him his arm.

"If your fingers start to go numb, tell us," I said.

We waited for a few minutes. Bert whistled for his horse, Simba. We heard her nicker at a distance. Bert whistled again. Her nicker was closer. Bert approached the sound slowly, murmuring nonsense sounds, trying to reassure the horse. She allowed herself to be captured. He led her to the road and mounted.

"Sorry we weren't able to stop 'em, Cap'n," Robby said. "Sure was fun, though."

"Speak for yourself," Bert said. "I didn't get to do a damned thing except get dragged on my ass."

"I gave as I got," Hank claimed. "He poked me. I poked him. Robby's right. 'Twas fun."

"I suggest you return by another gate," I said. "I'm sure our friends will tell the guards that they were attacked by brigands. If the one knows where he laced you, Hank, he'll tell the guards that, too."

"What about you, Cap'n?" Hank asked.

"I don't have time for a cross-country ride in the pitch dark," I stated. "I have an appointment to keep. I'll have to take my chances at the north gate. They'll be looking for four, with one wounded. I'll be alone, and I'm unharmed. I'll pretend to be a gent and act like I narrowly escaped the same fate. I'll work poor old Andy here into a fine lather. Thank you, men. The odds were against us tonight."

"They won't always be," Bert commented. "If you ever have a need like this again, Cap'n, I'd be delighted to take part."

"I hope I don't, Bert, but if I do, I'll send word," I promised.

The three of them decided the west gate was closer. They headed off the road. With a new moon and only starlight to guide them, it would be a slow trip. I headed back on the road. I could barely see it, but I trusted Andy could. When I judged we were about halfway back to the gate, I urged him to a gallop. I wanted Andy panting and sweating when we arrived.

When I could see the torches at the gate itself, I started yelling. "Ho! the gate! Ho! the gate! Help! Help!"

As I drew near the gate, I kept looking back over my shoulder as though the Lord of the Seven Hells himself were chasing me. Before I reached the light, I tried to mold my face into an expression of terror. I reined Andy in at the last possible moment before reaching the turnstile.

"Majors and Minors, help me!" I exclaimed.

Adopting my best facsimile of Freddy's cultured tone, I addressed the guards. "Let me in, damn your eyes! There's a group of four ruffians threatening to do me in. They've chased me the last few miles. I'm lucky to have escaped with my life!"

The guard sauntered over to the turnstile. He was in no hurry, enjoying my state of panic. He leaned on the weighted end of the pike, swinging it into the air.

I responded to his slowness with a 'harumph' and rode into the city. I picked my way through the dark streets, back to the Foaming Boar. I pulled up at the stable and dismounted. I gave a whistle, hoping the boy was near.

He was. He appeared out of the darkness. I handed him the reins.

"You gave Andy a nice bit o' work, sur," he commented. "Hain't seen him sweat like this afore."

"I did. He's a great horse," I added. "Saved my life tonight. Be good to him."

"I'll do that, sur. Give him a nice rub and brush and maybe a carrot."

It was just coming on eight o'clock. Entering through the kitchen, I was able to attract Carl's attention while remaining out of sight. I asked him to allow the cooks to give me dinner. Since one of them was within earshot and overheard, Carl merely nodded at him.

The cook ladled me a serving of beef stew and sawed a chunk of bread off a loaf. I took the bowl and a spoon and ate quickly. It was good stew. I used the bread to wipe the bowl when I finished.

I thanked the cooks and left by the back door. I walked toward the castle, wondering whether Sir Oliver would keep our appointment. Let me rephrase that. I knew Sir Oliver would be there. The question was whether he would help me or arrest me. I had previously thought him an honorable man. His behavior over the last three days had not been consistent with my previous impressions. It didn't much matter now. I was out of options and nearly out of time.

# 8

I reached a doorway where, hidden in the darkness, I could see the corner of Front and Bassett streets. There was a streetlamp there. While I was waiting for Sir Oliver, I was watching and listening for any indication that his men were assembling. I heard and saw nothing of the sort.

As a nearby clock began to strike nine, Sir Oliver walked into the pool of light at the corner. Reassured since I had not seen his men gathering to lie in wait, I left my doorway. I met him under the light.

"You're here," he commented. "I didn't know whether you would come."

"Sir Oliver," I replied, using his proper title for once, "you forced me into this. You have watched silently while du Pais and Albert have woven a story of half-truths and innuendo to paint me as a criminal, even though you know better. I no longer have any other cards to play. In order to clear my name, I must free the girl. No woman deserves the fate that du Pais has planned for Miss Traval. You know this as well as I. Are you going to help me?"

"I wish I could, Caz," he replied. "This is the most unfortunate episode I have ever experienced. The Crown ordered me to arrest you and charge you with the kidnapping four days ago. While I did bring you in, I let you go free, hoping you could find a way to resolve the matter before it came to this. They claim they just discovered Miss Traval in your rooms above the bookseller. I cannot help you."

"That's ridiculous, Ollie. I haven't been to my rooms in over a day."

"Nevertheless, they claim they discovered her there just now. She was bound and gagged. There are witnesses who say they saw you drag her in."

"Tell me, Ollie. Are we surrounded right now?"

"Yes."

"They've been in place a long time, then. I arrived early to see if I would spot them setting up."

"They've been here the better part of an hour," he explained.

"Too quiet and well-disciplined for City Watch," I commented. "Castle Shield?"

He nodded.

"Crossbows?" I asked.

He nodded.

I couldn't even draw my sword. Crossbow bolts would strike me down before it cleared the scabbard. I stood still, my disappointment and frustration washing through me. I looked at him, shaking my head sadly. I began to unbuckle my sword belt.

"Call them over, Ollie," I said as I handed him my sword.

Sir Oliver raised his right arm and made a beckoning gesture with his hand. I heard footsteps approach from all sides. My arms were seized from behind, and my hands were quickly tied. Sir Oliver handed my sword to one of the men. He turned and walked into the darkness.

Hands still grasping my upper arms shoved me in the direction of the gate. We went through. We crossed the small bridge. As we crossed, the portcullis lifted. We entered the castle, with the portcullis rattling down behind us. They shoved me to the right, down a torch-lit corridor. We reached a flight of stone steps on the left, leading down. Another left at the bottom and along another corridor. Straight ahead was an iron-barred door. Corridors extended to the right and left.

The guard behind the iron door unlocked it. They shoved me inside. The iron door shut with a clang.

I resolved to remind myself that even when things are horrible, they can always get worse. The guard searched me thoroughly to make sure I had nothing I could use as a weapon or a lockpick. Then he escorted me to a cell, the first one. The cells were on the left of the passage. The right was a sheer rock wall. He stopped me at the door and untied my hands. While he was doing that, I examined the cell. It was dry, an improvement over the last cell I stayed in, at the Palace of Justice. It seemed mostly clean, though there was a lingering odor of dead rodent and cat urine. There was a thin pallet of two sheets sewn together with something in the middle—probably straw. I was certain it was the home of all sorts of creepy-crawly things that would feast upon me when I tried to sleep. There were two buckets. One had a ladle, one did not. There was a short stool.

When he freed my hands, the guard asked me to get the bucket with the ladle. I did and handed it to him. He told me not to move. I heard water splash. He gave the bucket back. It was half-full of water. "Don't confuse the buckets," he warned.

He gave me a gentle shove. I heard the door shut and lock behind me. The light dimmed. There was a torch in the sconce opposite the door, but only a small opening at head level for light to enter.

With only an hour or so remaining before Viscount du Pais conducted his ritual, I knew I had failed. Even worse, I was accused of murder, kidnapping, theft and blackmail. Someone had been gathered a great deal of information on how I helped a handful of my previous 'clients' regain lost items. They used this information to paint me as an instigator of these thefts. At least three of the actual thieves had agreed to testify that they had taken their orders from me. They claimed they found Miss Traval bound and gagged in my rooms above the bookseller, with witnesses who claimed to see her enter. They accused me of the murder yesterday of the thug who attacked me two nights before, again with witnesses who claimed to have seen me kill him. I didn't know who 'they' were. The person who laid these charges at my feet was the one who had compelled me to investigate the matter, Sir Oliver West. I had believed he was worthy of my trust.

I tried to maintain a feeling of confidence that I could refute these charges. To do so would require the testimony of others of my 'clients'— people whom I had helped. By asking them to testify on my behalf, I would expose them to embarrassment, at least. In two cases, my clients would face divorce; in another, loss of his inheritance. They came to me because they heard I was discreet. What a mess.

To counter the kidnapping and murder charges would be easier. I had an alibi for the time of the murder. That would require me to ask Lord Rawlinsford to testify. Considering that the scandals surrounding me now had undoubtedly stained his reputation, that was a weightier request than it might have been. Freddy was an honorable man and would do it, but along with testifying that I was not a thief and blackmailer, it would probably be the end of our friendship. Our friendship would end because his family would not tolerate his association with me. The owner of the bookseller's shop would testify that Miss Traval had not been held in my rooms. His employees had stayed there the last two nights, keeping watch in case someone tried to burn the building down. That was the only charge I could prove false without damaging someone's reputation.

Whether I could win in court was immaterial, I realized. That would take time. I did not have time. I needed to find a way out of my cell—now.

That was impossible. The few people who knew where I was were not going to help. I sat down on the stool. I wasn't sure whether it was Bergeron or Albert, but one of them had outfoxed me.

I sat in the gloom. Sometime in the next hour, Bergeron, the Viscount du Pais, would conduct a black marriage. Following that ceremony, he and the people he had chosen to participate would rape the bride. They would finish by slitting her throat.

If Bergeron truly believed the ritual would gain him additional proficiency in the dark arts, he would have staged it in a temple to the Three Major Gods. Instead, he was using a shrine to the goddess of good fortune, here in the lower level of the castle. An innocent girl would suffer and die. Bergeron would gain power by tricking Albert, the Crown Prince, into being a willing participant in the rites. Bergeron would also be paid a million ducats due to the marriage contract with the girl's father.

The villain would win. I would be ruined. The reputations of people I had helped would be defamed. Altogether, a most unsatisfactory outcome. And here I sat, locked in a cell, powerless to do anything to stop it.

Self-pity is an indulgence I don't often allow myself. Here, the temptation was too great. The circumstances were too bleak. I wallowed in self-pity.

I heard some noise, but muffled by my door and the door to the passage itself, I couldn't tell what it was. I heard what I thought was the door to the passage open. Then the door to my cell began to open. I stood.

The open door revealed Wim, the younger brother of the Crown Prince. Wim was second in line to the throne. I also liked Wim, having served with him in the Rangers.

"Caz," he said breathlessly, "we have to hurry. The ceremony is about to start any second."

I was stunned that Wim knew anything about it. Freddy had told me he was unsuccessful in trying to reach Wim. To this point, there were only three of us who knew what was planned: My soon-to-be-former friend Freddy, his cousin Lucy and me. Sir Oliver West too, but he certainly had shown he was not on my side. Wim sensed my disbelief.

"Lord Rawlinsford told me all about it and begged me to stop it," he explained.

That had the desired effect on me. I allowed hope to flood my senses. Wim and I were going to prevent this horrible thing from happening.

"Follow me," he ordered.

I did. He left the passage and went into the main corridor. We turned left at the first corridor we reached. It ended in a T.

"Take this," he said. He handed me a short sword. The blade was just less than two feet long. The blade was wide and came to a sharp point. This is the type of sword that infantry use for close combat.

He pointed to the left. There was a corridor branching to the right that I could just see in the torchlight. "Go that way to the second door on the right. Wait there. I'm going over here." He pointed to his right. There was a corridor I could barely see that branched to the left.

"The shrine is immediately in front of us, on the other side of this wall. I'm going to the other side where I have some men waiting. We will burst in. When you hear us, enter from your side. We'll catch them in between us. Understand?"

I nodded. I grasped the sword and took off to take my position. When I reached the second door, it was already open a crack. I peered into the room.

Julienne Traval was naked. It was the first time I had seen her since she had left my rooms. By all that's Holy! Was it only four days ago? Someone had tied her hands with a length of rope. The rope was looped under the lip of the altar, stretching her arms over her head. Bergeron, in a black robe and black hood, was in the process of completing the job on her legs. Miss Traval was protesting feebly. Her squirming lacked strength. It was barely slowing Bergeron.

Obviously, the marriage portion of the program was complete. Bergeron was setting the stage for the despoiling. I saw Albert standing past her feet, fondling his erection hidden beneath a black robe. Where was Wim? He'd said he and his men would interrupt the ritual. I watched, waiting, as Bergeron finished binding her legs. When he hoisted himself on the altar, between her feet, and started pulling up his robe, I could wait no longer.

I opened my door with a slam, wanting to gain the attention of everyone in the room and, I hoped, Wim. Albert looked surprised. Bergeron did not. When he saw it was me, he bared his teeth in a feral grin.

"Perfect timing, bastard. Right on cue," he stated. "It is almost time for your part in our little ceremony."

"And what part is that?" I asked.

"Why, the part of murderer and dead man," Bergeron said, sliding off the table. "Though not in that order. I'm going to kill you first. Then Albert and I are going to have some fun with my new bride. When we're finished, we will put your own sword in your hand and have your dead hand cut her throat. I'll want you leaning over her, so the first powerful spurts of her blood coat your face and chest, providing proof positive that you performed the gruesome deed. Oh, we'll also blame you for her rape, you cretin, though you won't actually get to."

While he explained this, he had crossed behind the altar. On the other side, he bent briefly to pick something up. When he straightened, I could see it was my sword. He withdrew it from the scabbard as he continued around the altar. On the other end of the altar, Albert had also drawn a blade. He still seemed shocked by my appearance. Perhaps this was a part of the plan that Bergeron had not shared with him.

I didn't know whether Bergeron was any good with a sword. I did know that Albert was not, having seen him train in the Rangers. I also realized Albert must survive this encounter. I approached Albert quickly. He thrust at me. I stepped into him, blocking his thrust with my left hand. I felt the searing pain as the blade sliced my palm. At the same time, I swung my right fist, which was clutching the grip of the short sword I had. My fist connected with the side of his head. Albert fell like a marionette whose strings were cut.

Bending over, I dropped the short sword and quickly tugged Albert's blade from his hand. I did this just in time to parry a blow from Bergeron, who attempted to split my head in two. Bergeron followed this with another slash, a thrust, a feint and a thrust. He was good, and he was fast. It was all I could do to parry his blows while scrambling backward as quickly as I could. Lunge, thrust, feint, slash, thrust—his combinations were unpredictable, and all delivered from a position of perfect balance. He had me on the defensive. I was looking for an opening, a misstep, an over-extension, any sort of mistake I could use to turn things around. He did not make a mistake. He forced me all the way around the table.

I did not see Albert's unconscious form lying in my way. I could not take my eyes off Bergeron and the blade flashing in his hand—my blade, which irritated me. I was shuffling backward, and my left foot hit Albert. That threw me off balance for a fraction of a second. Bergeron thrust. I managed to parry just enough to redirect the sword from my guts into my left thigh. His success gave me an opportunity. My parry and stabbing my thigh caused him to extend just further than he anticipated. He was off balance by the barest amount. Needing to pull the sword out of my leg also slowed his recovery. That left me an opening. I buried Albert's blade up under Bergeron's chin and into his brain. He fell to the floor, dead. His dead hand yanked the sword from my leg as he fell.

This is when Wim and his men burst through the door. "Arrest that man!" Wim shouted, pointing at me.

I stood in complete disbelief. Two of his men ran to me. I dropped the sword from my hand. They seized me by the upper arms. I saw Wim reviewing the scene with a smug smile.

I could not make sense of it. They dragged me stumbling back to the cell. It took more effort for them since I had trouble putting weight on my left leg. They shoved me in and locked the door. Still confused by the turn of events, I realized I must see to my wounds. I sat on the low stool and stripped off my waistcoat and shirt. I began ripping my shirt apart to use it to bandage my hand and thigh. I peeled my breeches down and wrapped a sleeve from my shirt over the wound.

Bergeron had not hit anything vital. My thigh was still bleeding, but not at an alarming rate. I was careful not to wrap it too tightly—just enough to put pressure on the wound. My left hand, since I needed to use it, was bleeding more heavily. After wrapping it in the other sleeve, I was finished.

The adrenaline from the fight had worked out of my system. Now I was sitting shirtless, with my breeches pulled down to my knees. It was here that I realized things can always get worse since they had.

I didn't sit long. I heard commotion outside. My door opened and two members of the City Watch came in and hoisted me off the stool. They dragged me out. They did not give me the opportunity to make myself more presentable. My breeches were still down. They didn't care. They dragged me out of the cells, down a corridor, up a flight of stone steps, through another corridor and into the open air.

In the light of a few torches, I could see the prisoner wagon—an iron cage on top of a wagon. They bundled me in and locked the gate of the cage. A word to the driver and he started off. When we reached the streets of the city, I could feel every cobblestone. I clenched my jaw since the bumps made my teeth rattle. Some of the jolts knocked me into the bars.

I was grateful it was late. Common custom was to jeer any occupants of the prisoner wagon and throw garbage at them. The late hour meant the streets were almost empty, so I was spared that abuse.

They took me to the Palace of Justice. They pulled me out of the cage and dragged me inside and eventually down to a cell. They threw me in. Like the cell I'd been in a few days before, it was dark, dank and the stone floor was coated in some sort of slime. Shirtless, and with my breeches held up only by my boots, my body made intimate contact with that ooze. The feeling made me shudder in disgust.

I wish I could say my indomitable spirit prevailed. That's not the case. I hunched myself into a ball and sat there feeling sorry for myself. I wanted to curse. I wanted to cry. I did neither. When I had indulged my self-pity long enough, I tried to figure out Wim's appearance. Did he take advantage of the situation that presented itself, or was he somehow more involved? I wondered.

Later, I don't know how long; I heard the outer door being opened. The door to my cell opened. A figure stood there, with the guard behind. An old woman's voice barked orders.

"Get him out of this pisshole immediately," she commanded. "Put him somewhere clean and dry, with fresh air."

"Doctor," whined the guard.

She interrupted him before he spoke further. "Do you want infection to kill him before the court decides his fate? Are you saying your decision is more important than the magistrates'?"

Her voice was high-pitched and grating. Her tone, though, was commanding. She clearly expected instant compliance with her demand.

"Your decision is more important than the magistrates'?" she repeated. "Or you have no cells like that?"

"Doctor, but — "

"You do have cells like that," she stated. "Let me guess. You and the other guards use them to sleep when you're supposed to be on duty. Probably have proper beds in them, too."

"Doctor, you don't — "

"Take him to one of those now," she commanded.

Chastised, the guard replied, "Yes'm." To me, he jabbed his thumb in the air. "You. On your feet."

I struggled to my feet. The guard and doctor moved out of the door. I hobbled through.

"Help him, man," the doctor ordered. "Can't you see he's wounded?"

The guard reluctantly allowed me to put my left arm over his shoulder. We left this group of cells and went up a flight of steps. He paused and unlocked the outer door. We went through to the first cell on the right. As the doctor had guessed, it was clean and dry, equipped with a cot.

"Put him there," she demanded, pointing to the cot. When I sat down, she commanded, "Fetch some hot water. Be quick about it. I saw a kettle on the stove. Start with that. I'll want more, so put another kettle on the boil."

"Yes'm," the guard mumbled and left.

The doctor was wearing a cloak, carrying a small valise. I had not been able to see her face in the torchlight. It was shrouded by her hood. When the guard departed, she pulled the hood back. I recognized the pale blue eyes and unruly blonde hair even in the dim light. I gasped and was about to say something, but she put her finger to my lips to keep me silent.

"Hello, Caz," Lucy whispered in her normal voice.

The guard returned. He had poured the contents of the kettle into a bucket. He set the bucket down next to her.

"Come back with more hot water as soon as it's available," she ordered.

"Yes'm," the guard answered.

Lucy unwrapped the blood-stained make-shift bandages from my hand and thigh. She dipped a clean cloth she pulled from her bag into the hot water and began to wipe away the dried blood on my left hand. Finished with that, she began cleaning the wound itself. I winced, even though I tried not to.

"If you think that hurts," she whispered, "just wait."

When she had cleaned the slice in my hand to her satisfaction, she retrieved a bottle from her bag. She uncorked it. She held my hand out and poured the liquid onto the cut. Majors and Minors it hurt! I gasped. The liquid sizzled and bubbled in the cut.

"That's to reduce the chance of infection," she explained.

She then grasped a needle already threaded. Holding the edges of the cut together, she began stitching them. Her fingers moved quickly, but it still hurt. I endured it with clenched teeth, trying not to groan.

She withdrew some proper bandages from her bag and dressed my wound quickly and neatly. The guard returned with a fresh kettle. She directed him to pour it into the bucket. That done, he departed.

"Lucy," I hissed.

She stopped me. "Be quiet, Caz. Your voice carries," she whispered as she began to clean my thigh.

"We heard Wim apprehended you. Is he also the one who freed you from your cell in the castle?"

I nodded.

"I guessed as much," she said softly. "Freddy and I are trying to unravel all this, but we are baffled. They'll haul you into court tomorrow. Since you'll be charged with capital crimes for at least two murders, demand the King's Justice. That's your only hope."

An old custom in Aquileia was that people accused of murder or treason, which carried a sentence of death by hanging, could bypass court proceedings by demanding the King's Justice. Instead of a trial by jury, the accused could make his case directly to the king, with no lawyers allowed. It had last been invoked over a hundred years before and, if I recall correctly, the accused chose the option to speed things up. He preferred to face death immediately and not go through a trial that could drag on for weeks.

Lucy had been cleaning the wound in my thigh. She poured the liquid from the bottle into it when it was clean. Damme! It hurt. With the needle, she stitched it closed as well. She wrapped it with a suitable bandage. She then started wiping off the parts of me that had come into contact with the floor of the previous cell.

"You should be able to pull your breeches up over the bandage," she remarked when she finished.

It was only then that I realized her fingers had been within inches of my most private areas. My face flashed hot with embarrassment. She must have known. I swear I saw her eyes twinkle, even in the dim light.

"I'll have Freddy send Theo with clean clothes first thing tomorrow," she whispered. "You'll look somewhat presentable in court. Remember, demand the King's Justice."

She stood, retrieving her bag and pulling her hood back over her head. "I'm finished," she called to the guard, returning to the high-pitched voice she'd used earlier.

The guard came and collected her. He took the bucket she'd used. When they left, he shut and locked the door.

Lucy's visit had put wind back in my sails. I'd thought my friendship with her cousin was irretrievably damaged, and with it, any chance of exploring the strange connection I felt with her. Her appearance was a sign that all was not lost. How had she known to come to me or where to find me?

Stretching out on the cot, I began to think. When had Wim become involved? Had he learned of Bergeron's plan to compromise Albert and taken advantage of it? Or was Wim involved earlier? How early? Why would Bergeron go along with Wim's plan? My mind was a confused mess.

I tried to attack it from a different angle. What was the outcome Wim had desired most? The groundwork had been laid to portray me as the kidnapper. Bergeron had said that I was to be blamed for it all. Albert had seemed surprised by my entrance.

Wim's purpose was to compromise Albert and become the heir to the throne. Bergeron probably thought that helping Wim would give him the same leverage I had reckoned he would have over Albert. Albert probably thought he was going to gain magical power. Instead, he was the target—a more unwitting target than I was.

# 9

Morning came more quickly than expected. I had fallen asleep, pondering how I could have acted differently. I had charged headlong into this and made myself a convenient scapegoat by doing so.

When the guard came to give me a bowl of some variety of slop, their excuse for breakfast, he also tossed me a bundle of cloth. Neatly folded and tied together were a fresh shirt, breeches, stockings, underclothes and waistcoat. I put on the fresh clothing.

I had just finished dressing when I heard noises outside. I recognized the high-pitched voice of my 'doctor.' She waited for the guard to leave before lowering her hood and giving me a smile. She unwrapped my hand first. After inspecting the wound and the stitches, she put a new bandage on. Then she gestured for me to lower my breeches so she could see my thigh.

Before I did, I asked, "Is Albert alive?"

"Yes. Why?"

"I was worried Wim would have killed him."

"No. He's alive."

I breathed a sigh of relief. Then, I was acutely conscious of standing before her in just my underclothes. I chastised myself, telling myself not to react. I failed. To my great embarrassment, a part of me responded to her presence so close. My face grew hot and flushed.

Lucy attended to my wound. She examined the stitches and smelled the soiled bandages to learn if there was any putrefaction. Satisfied, she covered it with a fresh bandage and began to pull my breeches up. I stepped back and took over that task.

As she stood, she said, "Is that for me?" as she nodded at my now-distended underclothes. "Impressive. I'm flattered."

She may have been flattered. I was mortified. The Gods alone knew how many hours I had left on this earth. I hoped that would not be the lasting impression she had of me.

She managed to keep from laughing out loud at me. Lucy leaned forward and gave me a brief kiss. She raised her hood.

"I'm finished," she called to the guard.

He came and unlocked and opened the door. When she exited, he closed and locked it again. I could hear the outer door opening and closing.

There was something about Lucy that always left me with hope. The information that Albert was alive was a relief. It was a loose end that might help me unravel Wim's web of lies.

An hour or so later, I heard noises outside, with the outer door opening. When the door to my cell opened, there were four members of the City Watch there. I stood. One of them gestured me forward.

"Time to visit the magistrate," the one said.

They were carrying manacles. They pulled my arms back and fastened my hands together behind me. Another locked a pair around my ankles.

Two maintained position ahead of me. Two were behind me. All four were close. My left thigh burned with pain. I could only move at a slow, limping shuffle. The manacles around my ankles limited my stride. You could hear them clank with every step.

We left the cells and entered a wide corridor. People saw us coming and moved out of the way. I could hear conversations die as we approached and rise again after we passed. We reached the entrance hall of the Palace of Justice. The four members of the Watch led me to the central courtroom opposite the huge entrance doors.

They brought me in from the rear of the courtroom. That was unusual. Normally defendants were brought in from the side in a discreet way. They must have wanted to put me on display. The room was full of people. As I walked to the cage where those accused of crimes stood, I saw Freddy and Lucy among the spectators. When I entered the cage and turned to face the room, I saw Sir Oliver along the back wall. There were no empty seats. I did not see other faces I recognized, but clearly, this was a popular place to be.

In Aquileia, an accused criminal's first appearance before a magistrate took place before he or she was allowed to meet with a lawyer. It was a custom of long-standing. Aquileians believed it promoted speedier dispatch of justice.

The bailiff called the court to order and announced the magistrate. Everyone stood as he entered. I was already standing. Accused criminals were not given a seat.

The magistrate was a large man, tall and broad. His robes made him look even bigger. He swept in and took his seat at the head of the court. Once he sat, everyone else was allowed to sit. The magistrate had a flair for the dramatic. He took in the crowded room, gazing imperiously out over them. He slowly turned his eyes to me.

"Casimir FitzDuncan, you stand accused of murder, kidnapping, attempted rape, assault, blackmail, illegal entry to the Royal household and theft. Do you request a full reading of the separate charges before you make a plea?"

"No, milord," I replied in as clear a voice as I could muster from my suddenly dry mouth. "I demand the King's Justice."

An excited gabble rose in the court. More than murmurs, it started with loud gasps. The volume increased from there until a bellow from the magistrate rose above the noise.

"Silence!" he thundered. He did not stand completely but had raised himself from his seat. He turned to me.

"FitzDuncan, do you understand that your demand for the King's Justice eliminates your right to a trial by jury and permits you no legal representation?"

"Yes, milord. I understand. I demand the King's Justice."

"Very well. These proceedings are complete."

The magistrate stood. The court, once again buzzing, was slow to respond. He waited. Slowly, the audience realized and, group by small group, quieted and stood. When all were standing, the magistrate left. The members of the Watch who led me in now appeared in front of the cage. One unlocked it. They escorted me out the side door this time. I shuffled and clanked my way out.

Once again, conversation fell and rose along with my progress. They took me back to the cells. My thigh ached. When I reached the cell I had been in, I expected them to remove the irons. They did not.

"The irons?" I asked.

"They'll remove them at the castle if they want," said one with a chuckle. "Then again, they might decide you should keep them on."

They left. The guard locked my door. I sat on the edge of the cot to wait. The leg irons were ruining my boots but not hurting me. The ones on my wrists were digging in and rubbing my skin raw.

It wasn't a long wait. They came and collected me. They took me upstairs and to the prisoner wagon. It was mid-morning. This would be a far different trip than the one I took last night.

A crowd had already gathered outside, waiting for me to arrive. When they saw me exit the building, the jeering began. The guards hustled me aboard and locked me in. The wagon pulled away from the Palace of Justice.

The streets were busy. It was a normal day in the capital. People saw the prisoner wagon coming and stopped to look. Some gathered things to throw—whatever was close at hand. That meant rocks, garbage and even horseshit were hurled at me. Last night, through empty streets, they drove the wagon quickly. Today, with an audience to entertain, the driver took his time, moving at a slow walk. I protected myself as best I could. The garbage didn't hurt, but some of the rocks did.

The driver stopped at the gate in front of the bridge to the castle. He made a show of dismounting his perch and going into the guardhouse to ask permission to cross. This gave the crowd one final opportunity to hurl abuse and projectiles. He finally clambered back up and drove through. I was out of range of the garbage, but some strong-armed throwers were still tossing rocks. Past the halfway point of the bridge, it was safe to untuck myself from the ball I'd curled myself in.

The front of my shirt and the tops of my breeches were still clean since they'd been protected by my posture. The back of my shirt, my arms, my hair—pretty much anything that had been exposed—was filthy. I could smell rotted cabbage, horseshit and other unpleasant odors.

Through the portcullis, we entered the courtyard. The wagon stopped. Soldiers came and waited for the driver to unlock the cage. The soldiers actually helped me out of the cage. With a wounded thigh, my ankles chained and hands locked behind my back, jumping down would have been awkward at best. The leader of the group of soldiers, a sergeant I guessed from his bearing, asked the driver for the keys to the manacles.

The driver didn't have it. The leader of the soldiers began cursing at him. That made me more convinced he was a sergeant. Sergeants have a gift for cursing. After haranguing the driver thoroughly, the sergeant sent him on his way. He ordered a soldier to mount up, ride to the Palace of Justice, and retrieve the keys. He came over to me.

"This way," he said, pointing to a horse rail.

He strode over and leaned against it, indicating I should do the same. I shuffled after him. When I drew near, I thanked him for the opportunity to rest.

"Carl Stensland's my brother-in-law," he muttered softly. "Said he thinks you didn't do most of the things they tagged you with. I dunno about any of that—ain't my job. But I can show a little decency until it's all sorted, I reckon."

"Thank you, Sar'nt," I said.

It was some time before the rider returned with the key to the shackles. They unlocked them. The sergeant then ordered, "Strip."

I looked at him, puzzled. "You're covered in crap. We're going to hose you off. You'll be meeting with the king at some point. Can't have you smelling the way you do now. You should rinse your boots off, too."

I took off my clothes—somewhat reluctantly since I was in an open courtyard and the autumn breeze was chilly. The sergeant beckoned me to one corner. I saw four men beginning to work a pump, two on each side. Each side, in turn, pushed the handle on their side down. The sergeant picked up a canvas hose with a brass nozzle.

In a matter of moments, water began to squirt from the nozzle. He waited until it was more of a steady stream and aimed at me. The water, from deep in the well, was icy cold. It's hard to say which staggered me more, the force of the water or its temperature. I had trouble catching my breath. I tried to turn myself around, ending up doing a spastic sort of jig. I lowered my head into the stream to wash out my hair. He continued to blast me even after I thought I was clean enough. I think it was because I was providing entertainment to him and his men. He ended by hosing off my boots, blasting them across the flagstones.

He finished, and the men at the pump stopped. I was gasping. He beckoned me over to a bench.

"Take off the bandages," he instructed as he went in a door.

I sat and unwrapped my hand and leg. On his return, he was carrying a bundle and a roll of bandaging. He put the bundle down, then knelt to look at the wound in my thigh. After examining it, he took the bandaging and wrapped it. Then he did the same to my hand.

When he finished, he nodded at the bundle. "Clothes," he said. "Nothing fancy, but clean. Get dressed. Someone did a nice job stitching you up."

The bundle contained a blouse, loose pantaloons and stockings. They were made of homespun. The clothes were clean and simple but were not new. I dressed quickly, relieved to cover myself. I put my boots on last. They were wet, but the crud thrown at me had been rinsed away.

"Go with them," he ordered.

Two men walked me into the castle. They led me back down to where the cells were. They escorted me all the way into the cell—the same one as last night. They shut the door and I was alone again.

I tried to organize my thoughts. How would I present this fantastical story to the king? I would be accusing one son of being a fool and the other of being a criminal. I wasn't a father, but I imagined I would not react well if I were. I hoped the king would listen to what I said and not close his mind in reaction to it. Perhaps he would be grateful I asked for the King's Justice and kept the matter out of the courts.

One thing I did not know was whether the king would allow others to testify on my behalf. I doubted he would have the time or the inclination to do much in the way of investigating. Freddy told me they were able to paint me as the mastermind behind the theft of his ring, Pierre Luin's letters and Sir John Dunleavy's horse. Those were the first three people I had as clients. They did not mention any others. I wondered why not.

Freddy had referred both Pierre and Sir John to me. My fourth client, Lord Herron, had learned of me by overhearing a conversation between Freddy and Sir John. I didn't think Freddy knew any of my clients after Sir John. I doubted Freddy had been working with du Pais or Wim. I found it easier to believe he might have been indiscreet. It could have happened at any time in the past six years. If I were allowed visitors, and if Freddy came to see me, I would ask. He might not remember, though.

How to begin my narrative to the king? I suppose I ought to ask him if he were willing to hear it. If he were willing to be patient, I could start by telling him how I had helped people, beginning with Freddy. Then I could move to more recent events.

There was noise from outside. I heard the outer door open, and then my door was unlocked. When it swung open, both Freddy and Lucy were there. I stood. I wanted to speak, but emotion overwhelmed me. I was happy they came but felt as though I were about to sob.

"Freddy, dear, go ask the guard for something we can sit on," Lucy asked as she stepped toward me.

"Right," he said, heading out.

Lucy clasped me in a hug. Her arms went under mine and up my shoulder blades. My arms went around her waist. She laid her head on my chest. I could smell her hair. I couldn't place the scent, but it was perfect for her.

At first, I feared I would begin sobbing. Yet, the longer the hug lasted, the better I felt. I began to feel self-confident and assured.

When Freddy returned, holding two stools, he coughed quietly. Lucy released me, looking up at me as she did. What she saw on my face made her smile.

She had brought her small bag and wanted to inspect my wounds. She saw that my hand was freshly wrapped. "Who did this?" she asked.

"One of the soldiers," I replied. "After they hosed all the garbage from me, following a damned slow ride through the city."

"He did a fine job," she commented.

She wrapped the cut with a new bandage and beckoned me to stand. She yanked the pantaloons down before I could warn her I had no underclothes on. The blouse they'd given me almost covered everything, but not quite.

"Oops!" she exclaimed softly. "I'll be quick as I can, Caz," she said apologetically.

My shock and embarrassment, plus Freddy sitting right there, combined to prevent me from reacting the way I had before. Thank the Gods for small blessings! She finished quickly and wrapped my leg. Lucy pulled the pantaloons up where I could grasp them and I drew them back to my waist.

She noticed the scrapes on my wrists from the manacles. Lucy retrieved some salve from her bag and rubbed it in. Whatever was in it soothed the burning feeling.

"All done," she announced and tucked herself onto the stool Freddy had obtained for her.

"Have you met with the king yet?" Freddy asked.

"No," I replied. "I don't know when that will happen."

"Why did you ask for the King's Justice? No one has done that for years and years," he inquired.

"Lucy told me to," I answered.

Lucy gave me a pleased smile.

"And if Lucy told you to go hang yourself?" Freddy demanded.

"Now, look here, Freddy," I protested. "I didn't quite understand until I'd thought things through, but there are good reasons behind her advice."

Lucy favored me with another pleased smile.

"Such as?"

"Such as discretion," I explained. "If I need to call upon you, Pierre Luin and Sir John Dunleavy to respond to the accusations made, that I somehow arranged the thefts of the different items I retrieved for you, having to testify to the king is less damning than in the public proceedings of an open court. I know you've made your peace with what happened, but they might have different feelings. I may need to ask others as well. And since this involves both Albert and Wim, and I will show neither of them in a good light, I hope the king will appreciate that my choice will keep that out of the public eye."

"But you threw away your right to a trial by jury and can't have a lawyer assist you," Freddy protested, glaring at Lucy.

"Juries can be bribed or influenced," I said. "And I don't need a lawyer to tell the truth. I just need to hope I can present the information in a way that allows him to think as a king as much he will think as a father."

"Lucy," he growled. "What have you done?"

"I'm trying to save his life, cousin. As opposed to what you did," she snapped.

"What I did? What are you talking about? All I've done is try to help Caz in this mess," Freddy protested.

Lucy turned to me, her eyes looking as though they would spit flame in a moment. "Tell him, Caz," she demanded.

I knew what she was referring to. Damme! How does she know what I was thinking? I cleared my throat nervously.

"Freddy, when you met with Albert and Bergeron yesterday, they mentioned only you, Pierre Luin and Sir John Dunleavy in connection with me, correct?"

"I think so," he responded. "What does that have to do with anything?"

"You three were my first clients," I explained. "After Sir John, you don't know the names of any of my other clients, do you?"

Freddy leaped to his feet, indignant. "Are you saying I betrayed you?" he demanded.

"Not intentionally," I answered, trying to project calm with my voice. "By no means do I think you were working with du Pais and Wim or trying to help them."

"Then what are you saying?" he queried, his anger fading into worry.

"Is there a possibility that you might have been overheard talking about it sometime in the last six years? Late at night, with people you trusted?"

"No," he replied instantly.

"Are you sure, Freddy?" Lucy asked as she reached over and clasped his hand.

"I'm absolutely certain," he responded.

Yet, as I watched, I saw his face change. The grim set of his mouth began to turn to a look of dismay. Lucy let go of his hand.

"Majors and Minors," he breathed, incredulous. "I did. I just remembered. It was a few years ago, at the Metropolitan. We had been playing cards—you were Linc Ellsworth's guest. Ratty Hawkins was our fourth. You three had just left, and I was finishing my wine. Wim sat down with me. I was flattered he chose to join me. Among other things we discussed, he made a comment about you being a good sort—a pity you were a bastard. I agreed and told him how you had helped me, Pierre and Sir John out of our various jams. I'd forgotten all about it until just now. Oh, Caz. I'm sorry!"

"You're forgiven," I said immediately. "We all thought well of Wim. I did."

Lucy cleared her throat to get our attention. "If you will excuse me," she said. "I have to open the shop. I will return this evening to check your dressings, Caz."

"Thank you, Lucy," I said.

"I'll escort you out," Freddy offered.

"No need," she replied. "You two have things to discuss."

She came to me. After a brief kiss on the lips, she left. When she was gone, Freddy looked at me, his eyebrow cocked.

"She really likes you, you know," he commented.

I shook my head sadly. "Freddy, there's not much future there. I don't know that I'll ever see the light of day as a free man again. With the charges against me, there's a better than even chance they'll execute me in less than a fortnight. Then, even if I managed to clear my name, I'm still an illegitimate son. She's the daughter of the Duke of Gulick. Don't you—"

"She's the third daughter of the Duke of Gulick and the fourth of five children," Freddy interrupted. "The Duke is not wealthy. Her older brother will inherit the Duchy. Her younger brother has already been steered to a career as a lawyer. Her oldest sister had a fine dowry to cement her marriage to the neighbor's son. The next oldest sister was allowed to marry whomever she wished, but there was no dowry since the coffers were empty. She chose a young doctor in Haronberg. Like her, Lucy will be allowed to choose her husband."

"But it would be a scandal," I protested.

"Charles, the doctor, comes from a merchant family," Freddy stated. "Not a drop of noble blood in his veins. You, at least, are a son of the Earl of the Eastern March."

"Bastard son," I rebutted.

"Then marrying Lucy might ennoble you a bit, eh?"

"Don't joke, Freddy," I retorted. "Marrying me would drag her down to my level."

Freddy laughed. "You've only known her for a few days, Caz, but do you think she would care?"

I had to admit I didn't think it would matter to Lucy. She seemed to lack any sort of snobbishness. "Freddy, I've only known her for, what? Three days? Four, now? For that reason alone, it's ridiculous to talk about it. Besides, I need to focus on how I'm going to explain all this to the king. If Wim has his ear, I'm as good as dead already, no matter what I say."

"Lucy is confident you will pull through this," Freddy said. "That gives me some hope."

"I wish I could share that feeling," I remarked.

A strange thought occurred to me then. "It's funny, Freddy. While Lucy was here, I felt confident I would prevail. Now that she's gone, I don't."

"Remember when you asked me if I believed she was a witch?" Freddy asked. "And I told you sometimes I did? This is one of those sometimes. She *made* me remember that conversation with Wim, Caz. I'm convinced of it. I doubt I would have remembered it on my own. It was idle conversation, late at night—completely unimportant at the time."

"Wim obviously remembered it," I pointed out.

"I already said I'm sorry," Freddy complained.

"I didn't mean it that way," I countered.

"Caz, what exactly happened since I saw you last?"

I recounted to Freddy about riding out of town and our failed attempt to intercept the carriage. Next, I described my meeting with Sir Oliver near the castle gate.

"Huh," I muttered in the middle of describing this.

"What?"

"I suspected Sir Oliver was taking his orders from the Crown. I'd thought it was Albert. It wasn't. It was Wim. I wonder if Sir Oliver knew what Wim had planned?"

"Does it matter?" Freddy asked.

"It might. Sir Oliver arrested me the night Miss Traval was kidnapped. He said it was on orders of the Crown. He knew at the time that I could not have kidnapped the girl. He maneuvered me into investigating her disappearance and let me go. Was that part of the plan? Or was it an unexpected wrinkle?" I mused out loud.

Freddy started to speak, but I held up my finger to silence him. I needed to think. If I'd stayed in custody, what would have happened? How would the final scene have unfolded? I would not have been in the shrine. Wim would have burst in and interrupted. Why would Bergeron go along with that? He would become the scapegoat—guilty of kidnapping his own fiancée and planning the obscene ritual. He would never have agreed to that, meaning I was meant to be released.

Sir Oliver had almost forced me to look into the girl's disappearance. Wim knew that any attempt at investigation would have me call at Traval's offices and upon Madam Traval. That could be used against me. Why was I attacked twice? I'd reacted as a horse does to spurs—that was the point. The attempt to capture me after we met Madam Traval? My escape had no bearing. Wim developed another plan to pull me in. I was supposed to be in a cell in the castle, where Wim could free me. He knew I would not let them kill the girl. Had it worked out to Wim's satisfaction?

"It would have been better if I also killed Albert," I said out loud.

"What!?!" Freddy asked.

"Sorry," I said. "My mind has been racing. Let me explain."

I shared my thoughts with Freddy, from Sir Oliver releasing me onward. Then I reached the events following my capture. "I was meant to be in this cell so that Wim could 'free' me," I explained. "He planned for me to burst into the room to stop any further harm to the girl. I knocked Albert unconscious, then killed du Pais. It would have been better for Wim if I had killed Albert as well. Perhaps he thought I did. It would be interesting to see what sort of view of the room he would have had."

Freddy looked confused.

"Wim had a different story prepared depending on what happened. All of them end with Albert being dead or compromised. Freddy, I need to ask a favor of you."

"What?"

"I need you to speak with Albert privately. You need to get him to speak with me. He won't want to. He thinks I'm a lower form of human due to my birth status. Share as much of this as you understand with him."

Freddy left. I hoped he would be successful in convincing Albert to speak with me. Otherwise, Albert would lose the throne and I would lose my life.

The guard came and gave me a chunk of bread for lunch and asked me to check my water bucket. There was still plenty. The bread was good, still slightly warm. The crust was thick and chewy, the inside surprisingly heavy.

As I gnawed on it, I reviewed in my mind the best opening to my meeting with the king. If Wim were there, could I request that he leave? Having him sit in the meeting would guarantee my death.

My mind wandered to thoughts of Lucy. I tried to wrestle it back, but just like my feet had taken me to her shop against my will, my mind kept returning to her. By now, I was certain she was a witch of some sort. Like Freddy, I believed she had helped retrieve the memory of his conversation with Wim. When I was in her presence, I felt… it was hard to describe, other than to say I felt better. She restored my self-confidence. I was less confused when she was near and could think more clearly. Though we had only exchanged a few chaste kisses, my lips tingled at the memory.

I started to wonder about the extent of her abilities but found myself thinking instead of her smile, her pale blue eyes, her freckles, her unruly hair, and the way she smelled. Realizing I'd lost focus, I tried to concentrate on the magical talent she had displayed. Again, I found myself distracted, thinking about how she'd felt in my arms when she hugged me. I almost laughed out loud. Preventing too close an examination was probably one of her abilities. It's why Freddy said he always talked himself out of thinking she was a witch and why I couldn't think about it now.

I sat and tried to think of nothing at all. Staring at the torch outside the small window in the top of my door gave me a focus. I was able to clear my thoughts. Once my head was empty of images of Lucy, I tried to review different approaches I might make when I met the king. It all depended on reading his mood. If he were willing to listen, if his mind was made up already, if he would be patient—all these would determine which opening would be best.

The rest of the day wore on. I grew tired of trying to guess what sort of mood the king would have. I felt like a dog chasing his tail. My sense of frustration gave me nervous energy that I had no way to expend. The cell was too small to allow me to pace. I went back to staring at the flame of the torch.

There was noise outside. The guard entered shortly after. He opened the door of the cell and handed me a bowl, a spoon, and another hunk of bread. The bowl contained a thick fish chowder. It was vastly better than the slop they served me in the Palace of Justice.

As I was mopping the sides of the bowl with the last of the bread, the guard appeared with Lucy. I handed him my empty bowl and spoon and thanked him. When he turned his back on us, Lucy embraced me as she had earlier. The same feeling her hug had given me earlier in the day, of self-confidence and assurance, flooded through me.

She released me and bent to check my wounds. Once again, she yanked my pantaloons down. This time, without Freddy in the room, I reacted to her close presence. She did not say anything but gave me a wink when she was finished replacing the dressing on my thigh. She checked my wrists and applied more of the salve.

"They'll scab over tonight," she said. "Don't worry about it. It's part of the healing process."

She sat on a stool. Reaching into her bag, she retrieved two pieces of paper, folded and sealed. "These are for you," she said.

"What are they?"

"One is a sworn statement from Lyle Forteney. He declares that Miss Traval was never held in your rooms above his shop. His assistants spent the last three nights there, keeping watch. The other is a sworn statement from Lord Rawlinsford, in which he affirms that you could not have committed the murder of Algernon Toohey, as you were in his presence the entire time."

I had not mentioned either of these to Freddy or Lucy. How had she known? I looked at her, questioning. She returned an expression of feigned innocence.

She rose from the stool. "I'll return in the morning with some of your clothes."

"Can you bring my razor and a tooth stick?" I asked. "I haven't been able to shave or clean my teeth since I woke up at Freddy's."

"I doubt they'll let you have a razor," she answered. "They'll let me shave you, though. I'll bring a comb as well. Oh! I almost forgot. Freddy was able to meet with Albert after he left you."

"What was their conversation?" I asked eagerly.

"Albert was resistant," she reported. "What information Freddy shared with him was contrary to what Bergeron had told him. He also had difficulty accepting that Wim was involved, let alone that Wim hoped to supplant him in the succession. Freddy did not try to change his mind. He asked Albert to think about what he'd shared, then left."

"That was probably a good strategy," I acknowledged. "I have a question. Do you know anything about the rules of the King's Justice?"

"No, but I have a law book," she said.

"I'm worried that Wim will try to be present during my meeting with the king. I want to know if I can prevent that."

"I'll check and let you know what I learn tomorrow morning."

"Thank you. And please thank Freddy as well."

She came to me, rose on her toes, and gave me a kiss. My lips tingled as she left. I sat and looked at the letters she had given me. They would disprove two of the crimes of which I was accused. I still had a long way to go in order to prove my innocence, but they were a start.

Once again, seeing Lucy restored my spirits and confidence. Realizing it was Temple Day, I'm not ashamed to admit I muttered a quiet prayer to the Majors and Minors, thanking them for putting Lucy and Freddy in my life. Then I made separate prayers to the goddess of fortune, the goddess of wisdom and the goddess of love, asking for their help both sooner and later.

# 10

I returned to staring at the torch (hey—there was nothing else to do). When I was considering leaving my stool to lie down on the thin pallet on the floor, I heard the outer door open. My door swung open. Albert stood behind the guard in the corridor.

"Go," he ordered the guard.

"Hand me a stool," he told me.

I did. He set it in the corridor and sat.

"Sit," he said.

He looked at me with an expression I couldn't figure out. It seemed to have elements of distaste, desperation, embarrassment, and both fear and hope. I didn't say anything, waiting for him.

"Lord Rawlinsford told me some things earlier today that disturb me. I was not listening carefully since I did not want to believe some of what he said. He told me you know more. I'm here to ask you some questions."

I nodded.

"Tell me what you know of this mess."

I took a deep breath and began. He let me tell the story. When I explained that there had been no possibility of gaining any magical ability from the Viscount's ritual—that its entire purpose was to compromise him, he winced slightly. I told him why Wim had involved me—to be a pawn on which blame could be fixed.

When I finished, I asked, "Your Highness, has your brother spoken to you and suggested that you provide an alternative explanation to your father for why you were in the shrine? Did he advise you to say that you and he worked together to prevent this dreadful ritual from taking place? That you should tell your father Bergeron and I were the perpetrators?"

Surprise was evident on his face. "He did."

"Your Highness, I am sure that he will talk to your father soon if he has not done so already. He will tell him the real reason you were there and the lie which you plan to tell. When I meet with your father and tell him what I've now shared with you, what do you think will happen?"

"Father will think I'm a fool and a liar, unworthy of the throne. He will disinherit me in favor of Wim. My brother will convince him I am a threat and they will have someone kill me. I will die in an unfortunate accident, I expect."

"Your Highness, do you see a way out of the trap your brother set?"

His face screwed up in distaste, as though he had bitten into a lemon. He deliberated silently. His expression did not change.

"I will have to tell father I'm a fool, but fortunately not a criminal or a liar. He will then need to decide between a fool and a schemer. Tell me. Why are you helping me? Is this another layer to this plot?"

"Your Highness, it is not another layer to the plot. I'm fighting for my life. If I help you in the process of clearing my own name, so be it. You have always treated me with contempt. But you have never put me into a position where I would be blamed for crimes I did not commit, using my illegitimacy to cement the charges against me."

Albert nodded and rose. Following protocol, I stood as well. He walked to the entrance door and called the guard, leaving the stool in the corridor. After letting Albert out, the guard locked me in again. I lay down on the thin pallet and tried not to think about the bugs that would feast on me that night. I fell asleep before I felt any bites.

Morning seemed to come early. The guard, checking on me, tossed me a large chunk of bread. Warm from the oven, it was tasty, wholesome and filling. Lucy arrived not long after. As promised, she brought clothes, a comb and a tooth stick. She checked my wounds and bandaged them with fresh dressings. She put more salve on my wrists. She stepped out then.

When she returned, she had a bowl and a razor. She entered my cell, and the guard shut and locked the door behind her. "He agreed to allow me to shave you," she explained. "When I'm finished, I have to pass the razor through to him before he will let me out."

I nodded to the guard, watching through the small opening in the door. "Thank you," I told him.

Lucy had me sit. From her small bag, she retrieved a cloth and a small piece of soap. She wet the cloth in the bowl of water and then rubbed it on the soap. When she had a lather, she began to rub it over my face.

The water was not hot, but I didn't mind. Lucy took the razor and began scraping the whiskers from my face. Her touch was light and sure. It almost felt like a caress. When she finished, she wiped the remaining soap away. She rinsed the razor in the bowl, stood, and gave it to the guard through the door opening.

He disappeared, taking the razor outside. He returned and unlocked my cell. Lucy stepped out to give me the opportunity to change. She had brought a complete set of clothing, including a cravat and waistcoat. I dressed quickly, relieved to be in normal clothing. Lucy came back in with comb in hand.

I tried to tell her I could comb my own hair, but she insisted on doing it. Again, her touch was sensual. I'd never viewed combing my hair as anything more than necessary, but under Lucy's hands, it was extremely pleasurable. She gave me the tooth stick I'd requested. Looking at it, she'd dipped it in some sort of substance. I looked at her, questioning.

"From my shop," she explained. "It will make your teeth cleaner and your breath fresh. Rub it on your teeth and tongue."

I busied myself for a moment, cleaning my mouth. The substance on the stick dissolved in my saliva. I did as she instructed. When I finished, she handed me the water ladle and told me to rinse my mouth, then spit the water out.

Once I'd finished that, she stepped to me. "Let me check to see if you did a good job."

She grasped my head in her hands and pulled me down into a kiss. Our lips met. She opened her mouth slightly. I felt the tip of her tongue trace my lower lip. Caught up in the sensation, I sent my tongue to greet hers. They played together for a moment. Then she pulled herself away, panting slightly.

Though my heart was pounding, I worried that I had taken liberties with the lady. I was on the verge of apologizing, but she spoke first. Her face was flushed. She gazed at me from hooded eyes as she whispered, "This is neither the time nor the place, Casimir FitzDuncan, but I swear to you there will be both a time and a place to explore that further."

She embraced me in a hug, her head on my chest. We both caught our breath. When she released me, she stepped back.

"I checked the law books I have. There isn't much on the King's Justice," she said. "It does say neither of you is allowed to have counselors in the room when you meet. I would imagine the king is allowed bodyguards, but it was not mentioned in the books."

"Thank you. That may prove to be enough if Wim attempts to join the meeting. Thank you for the clothes, the shave, for… Majors and Minors! Thank you for everything, Lucy."

"You're welcome," she replied with a smile.

She gathered her things and left. Once again, Lucy's presence had filled me with confidence. The positive energy stayed with me until a group of guards came to collect me. When they put manacles on my hands, behind my back, and then my ankles, the confidence dissipated.

They marched me out, two in front and two behind. I shuffled and clanked. The weight of the leg irons made my injured thigh ache. We climbed to the main floor. Turning a corner, our group encountered Albert. As we passed him, he ordered the guards to stop.

"Take those off," he said.

"Your Highness?" the leader asked.

"Tale those off," Albert repeated.

"Your Highness, he's a criminal," the leader explained.

"He's an unarmed man, wounded. Do you think he's so fearsome that he can overpower the four of you? Take those off."

The leader of the group clearly did not know what to do. He did not want to disobey Albert. Someone had given him orders to put me in chains.

"If you are afraid of him, I will escort him by myself," Albert said.

"Yes, Your Highness."

The leader nodded to the man with the keys. He unlocked my hands and ankles. Once Albert saw it was done, he grunted and continued on his way.

They led me to a room. There was a long table with chairs surrounding it. The leader pointed to a chair in the middle of the near side and told me to sit. The four guards arranged themselves behind me against the wall.

The king entered, followed by Wim. Wim was wearing my blade. That annoyed me, but I swallowed my feelings as best I could. I stood and bowed to the king. He sat.

"Your Majesty," I said. "I don't know much about the proper procedures of the King's Justice, except this—neither of us is allowed counselors. I respectfully ask that His Highness leave us."

"Father," Wim hissed. "The King's Justice is whatever you decide. This man will spin a web made entirely from lies. I can tell you when he is lying."

"I think I am qualified to know when a man is lying, Wim. If I am unsure, I promise I will discuss it with you later. He has a valid point—he is allowed no counsel. I think it is fair that I should do without as well."

"You're making a mistake, father," Wim muttered angrily.

"Perhaps," the king admitted in a calm tone. "I don't believe I must make any decision today, though. I will make a judgment only after I am sure it is the correct one. If I need your assistance in sorting through things, I will be able to obtain it. You should leave."

"Father, you don't know how clever this man is," Wim protested. "He will convince you that black is white and white is black."

"Then it should be a most entertaining discussion," the king answered. "You may leave now."

Wim did not move at first. Just as his delay was beginning to feel awkward, he sighed dramatically. He heaved his chair back and stood. He turned towards the door. When he was out of his father's line of sight, he threw a menacing look at me.

When the door shut, the king looked at me. "Casimir FitzDuncan, there is a list of charges against you that is appalling. According to what I've been given, you have committed two murders, a kidnapping, extortion, blackmail, assault and theft. I presume you will tell me you are innocent of all these crimes."

I thought quickly. "Your Majesty, I have prayed that you would listen to what I have to say with an open mind. Your willingness to dismiss your son from our meeting gives me hope that you will. I must also beg for your patience since it will take time for me to explain to you what I know. As for my innocence or guilt, I requested the King's Justice. That will be for you to decide."

"A thoughtful answer," he affirmed. "Why don't you begin. If I feel you are wasting my time, I will stop you."

I took a deep breath. For my starting point, I chose the same incident with which I opened my account to you. He allowed me to continue with few interruptions. His first was when he asked me to repeat what Sir Oliver had told me as the reason for my arrest. I repeated what Sir Oliver had said about the matter rolling downhill to him.

He nodded and bade me continue. When I reached the point where the two letters I had been given were relevant, I handed them over. I arrived at the time in the narrative when I met Sir Oliver and the Castle Shield arrested me. The king held up his hand to stop me.

"Would you care to eat?" he asked. "I just heard the bells of mid-day. I sense your narrative is reaching a climax. I would like to pause while I consider what you have said. Plus, I'm hungry."

He did not wait for my response. He stood. I quickly rose. He left the room but returned moments later.

When he sat, he said, "I know your father and knew your grandfather. You take after your grandfather more."

"Thank you, Your Majesty. If I am favorably compared to him, that is high praise. He gave me the sword I saw on your son's hip this morning."

"I thought I recognized it," the king muttered to himself. "If I decide to clear your name, I will see that it is returned to you."

They delivered meat pie. Servants swept into the room, set places in front of us, then served us. They brought a flagon of water. I drank thirstily—talking as much as I had, gave me a dry mouth. The strangeness of the situation occurred to me. Here I was, accused of terrible crimes, eating politely with the king.

When he finished, the servants reappeared and took everything away. They were efficient and graceful. It took only moments.

The king leaned back in his chair and motioned for me to resume my story. I recounted the events from the time Wim released me from my cell. When I reached the shrine, the king interrupted me.

"What happened to the guard outside your cell?"

"I don't know, Your Majesty. I did not see him, though I will admit I did not look closely. I assumed Wim had sent him away."

"Continue," the king said.

When I finished, he asked if there were any other things I wanted to share with him. I told him about the conversation Albert and I had last night. The king nodded.

"You have given me a great deal to consider," the king told me when I finished. "You may go."

I stood and bowed, then backed around my chair towards the door. The king also rose and walked briskly out of the room. When he left, I turned to face the guards. The leader opened the door, and they escorted me back to my cell. Neither Freddy nor Lucy visited that night or the following days.

With nothing to do, my mind raced. I remembered all sorts of things I should have said or said differently. I worried and fretted. I argued with myself whether the delay in the king's decision was a good thing.

On the third day after meeting with the king, just past mid-morning, the guard opened my cell. A page was waiting outside. My hopes climbed since my escort was a page and not armed soldiers. He took me to a different part of the castle. He knocked on a closed door.

"Enter!" came a voice.

The page opened the door and said, "Casimir FitzDuncan, Your Majesty."

The king was sitting behind a desk strewn with papers. I saw my sword lying across some of the papers. I bowed.

"Your Majesty," I said.

"I believe this is yours," he said, indicating my sword.

"Yes, Your Majesty."

"Go ahead. Take it. Don't put it on until you leave the room, though, or Jared here will react poorly," he said, jabbing his thumb at the guard standing behind him.

"Thank you, Your Majesty," I said.

As I picked up my sword, he added, "You're free to go. Please observe your normal discretion regarding all these events. I've already asked the same of Lord Rawlinsford and Lady Darling."

"Of course, Your Majesty. And thank you."

"I hope our next meeting is under more pleasant circumstances, FitzDuncan. Good day," he said.

I backed to the door. Thankfully, the page was still waiting. When he shut the door behind me, I buckled on my blade.

"Can you show me the way out?" I asked.

"Certainly, sur," he replied.

I followed him to the main courtyard outside the entrance. Majors and Minors, the sun felt good upon my face. It was a beautiful fall day, without a cloud to be seen. I took a deep breath of the fresh air and left the castle.

# 11

I decided my first stop would be my rooms. After so many days in cells, I wanted a bath. Many of my prayers had been answered. The king listened to what I told him with an open mind. The truth won out, cutting through the complex web of half-truths that Wim had woven.

"Mr. Forteney," I called out as I entered the bookseller. "I want a hot bath, please. Can you see to it?"

"Oh, Mr. Fitz, I'm going to have to add it to your rent," he replied.

"Now, now, Mr. Forteney, my contract states quite clearly that you are to provide me with one hot bath per week at no additional cost to me," I responded, wagging my finger.

"But Mr. Fitz, that's two times in a row that you've demanded a bath on a weekday. Your regular day is Saturday and today is only Friday."

"Mr. Forteney, how many baths did I have last week?" I asked.

"One," he responded.

"How many this week?"

"You haven't had any."

"The contract, Mr. Forteney—the contract that you drew up with painstaking attention to detail—states you are to provide me one hot bath per week. It does not specify which day. I agreed to Saturday since you claimed it would be the easiest day for you to provide it. I did that out of the goodness in my heart, Mr. Forteney, since the contract allows me to demand my bath on any day. If I ask for another bath tomorrow, then you may charge me. Just to warn you, Mr. Forteney, after the week I have had, I might demand a hot bath every day."

"Then I shall have to charge you, Mr. Fitz."

"For a hot bath tomorrow, Mr. Forteney, I would not attempt to avoid responsibility for that fee. Yet, if I demand a hot bath Monday, you shall not charge me."

"Damn your sharp eyes, Mr. Fitz," he said with good humor. "Sur, I will word the next contract more carefully. It's a terrible thing to be subject to a young man's whimsy."

We were both smiling as I headed to the stairs at the rear of the shop. This was the type of exchange with which we entertained the staff and amused ourselves. Upon entering my rooms, I could see they were spotless. The clothing I had given to Placida was wrapped in paper and string. Taking the bundle into my bedroom, I opened it. Placida had managed to save the clothes I had smeared in the slime of the cell floor. I made a mental note to pay her a little extra this week.

As I was stowing the clothing in the armoire, I heard a knock on the door. "Hallo, Caz," came Forteney's voice. I bade him enter as I went to meet him.

"All's well that ends well," he commented.

"Aye," I replied. "Thank you for the letter."

"Tweren't no trouble," he said. "Especially since it was Lady Darling who asked me. Tell me, Caz. Is she really a Lady? Lady Darling sounds like a name an actress makes up for herself."

I couldn't hold back my snicker. "I will have to tell her that. Lady Darling is the daughter of the Duke of Gulick."

"Please don't tell her I said that," he asked. "So, what was all this about?"

"Lyle, you know I won't tell you," I replied. "I'll just say it was complicated and I'm lucky to be standing here right now."

"Fair enough, Caz. Fair enough," he said as he left.

The boys were bringing up the buckets of hot water. I waited for them to fill the tub while I prepared what I needed on a low stool next to the tub. A cloth, soap, and my razor. Then I stripped eagerly. I unwrapped my bandages and grabbed a cloth and some soap from the shelf. Stepping in the tub, the water was the perfect temperature—hot, but not excessively. I let out a sigh, and it felt as though my whole body sighed. It felt as though I was washing away not only the physical filth but the emotional scum as well.

I washed my hair last. My knees stuck out of the water when I slid down in the tub to submerge my head and work my hair with my fingers to remove the last of the dirt and soap. When I lifted my head from the water, I blinked to clear my eyes. Lucy was perched on the stool, sitting next to the tub. Her chin was in her hand, with her elbow resting on the knee of her crossed leg. There was a definite twinkle in her eye.

"Well, hello, Lucy. Let yourself in. Make yourself at home," I said as I covered my groin with the small scrap of cloth I'd been using to wash.

"Why, thank you, Caz. I think I will," she responded. She looked into the water at the small cloth. A smirk was on her lips.

I noticed she was not dressed in her usual flowing garments. She was in the latest fashion. The dress was a blush color. It was tight in the bodice, displaying a hint of decolletage, with a flowing skirt. Her hair, usually loose and free, was tamed and gathered neatly at her neck, draped over her left shoulder. She wore a small, stylish hat, cocked to the left. Though I was tempted to comment, I held my tongue. To me, Lucy was beautiful in whatever she chose to wear.

"I came to check on your stitches," she said. "They kept me away the last three days, so I haven't been able to check your wounds. Any problems?"

"No."

"It's a good thing you've been soaking," she commented. "It will make it easier to remove the stitches. Now, if you don't mind standing?"

"Lucy, if you would be so kind as to hand me a towel from the shelf behind you, I would appreciate it."

She stood and retrieved a towel. She turned and handed it to me. I waited for her to move. She did not, remaining there with a smirk. She was teasing me and I knew it. This time, instead of embarrassment, I was growing excited.

"Lucy, much as you are enjoying yourself, it's time for you to turn your back to me so I can stand up."

"Oh, poo!" she said, not mad at all. "I'm having such fun, too."

She did turn around, though. I quickly wrapped the towel around my waist. It's a good thing I didn't delay because she turned back before I invited her.

"That's disappointing," she said when she saw I'd covered up. "Though I do notice you are glad to see me."

I looked down. My swelling was evident under the towel. "A beautiful and charming lady come to visit me in the bath—why shouldn't I be happy?"

She took my hand. "Come over here into the light and let me look... at your stitches," she said with a giggle.

She looked at my hand first. After nodding approvingly, she went to her bag and got a small pair of scissors. She snipped the stitches and then plucked them out, one at a time. It had hurt when she sewed them. Removing them did not hurt at all.

She then knelt down to examine my thigh. Using the scissors, she clipped those stitches as well and removed them. She did not tease me in the process, for which I was grateful. She stood when she finished.

"There's no reason to continue to wrap these," she explained. "Better to let them breathe." She then shoved me in the direction of my bedroom.

"Get dressed, Caz. We're having lunch with Freddy at the Equestrian Club. It struck mid-day while you were under water. We are both eager to speak with you."

As quickly as I could, I dressed for the type of day Lucy mentioned. I found a pair of boots that were still acceptable, though worn. The boots I'd worn home had scuffs on the ankles from the leg irons and I did not want to display them in public. I also had no money pouch. I went to my strongbox and withdrew 20 ducats and wrapped them in a handkerchief, which I then placed in my pocket.

Finished, I opened the door and presented myself for inspection. I don't know why I did. It seemed like the right thing to do. Lucy looked me over carefully. She adjusted my cravat and tsked at my boots.

"After lunch, Lucy, please remind me that I need to purchase new boots and a money pouch," I asked.

"I won't forget," she replied.

I allowed her to precede me down the stairs. When we reached the alley, I offered her my right arm. She tucked her left hand into my elbow. She had put on gloves on the way down the stairs, I noticed.

"Lucy, you look lovely today," I said. "You look lovely every day, but I noticed you are dressed differently. "

She smirked at me. Her smirk was getting a lot of use today. "What day is tomorrow, Caz?"

"Saturday," I replied.

"How clever of you," she stated dryly.

I was missing something. I tried to think. Saturday… Fall… Women dressing up… My eyes widened and my mouth fell open.

"Queen's Cup?" I asked.

"That's better," she said.

"I completely forgot," I admitted.

"You've had other things on your mind," she offered.

"You can say that again."

"You've had other things on your mind."

Her eyes twinkled, and she laughed. Her laugh has such a sweet timbre. I couldn't resist laughing myself.

"You're taking me," she announced. "We'll be sitting in the family's box."

I stopped. A thousand insecurities rushed through my head. Her family's box meant parents. It would be a moment of reckoning. I chose my next words with care.

"Are you sure that's a good idea?" I asked.

"It's not just a good idea," she said. "It's imperative. And, I'll have you know, while you were indisposed, I took the liberty of studying the contents of your armoire. I found your wardrobe lacking. After lunch, you are buying new boots and a money pouch. You are also buying a new pair of breeches, stockings, a shirt, cravat, waistcoat and jacket. I've already chosen the fabrics and your tailor is waiting for us. You'll be paying extra since it's a rush job."

"Considering I wasn't released until this morning—don't you think you were taking a gamble?"

"Perhaps," was all she said.

We resumed walking. "These new clothes I am buying — "

"Will complement the fabric of my dress," she said. "It *is* the Queen's

Cup."

I believe I mentioned the Queen's Cup earlier in this tale. It's the premier steeplechase race in the kingdom. The last race of the season, it is also one of the most significant social events of the year. It is the last opportunity for people to see and be seen before the cold winter weather arrives and forces everyone indoors.

"Please excuse my puzzlement, Lucy," I said. "This is catching me off balance."

She laughed. "You've had other things on your mind. There. I said it again."

We reached the Equestrian Club. We checked in with the major domo and informed him we were guests of Lord Rawlinsford. He assigned someone to take us to him.

Freddy had booked a small private room. When we entered, he stood. After giving Lucy a kiss on the cheek, he clasped my hand in both of his.

"I'm glad to see you, Caz."

After we sat, he quizzed me. "Tell us what happened since we last saw you."

"There's not much to tell, I'm afraid. The evening before I last saw you, Lucy, Albert came to talk. He mentioned he had spoken with you, Freddy. He wanted to hear my side of things. I told him what I knew and what I believed. After you left the next morning, Lucy, I had my interview with the king. It lasted through lunch. When we finished, they took me back to my cell. I remained there until they took me to the king this morning. He returned my sword to me and asked me not to discuss what had happened. That's all I know."

Freddy leaned back in his chair when I finished. "Lucy and I can add a little to your understanding," he said. "I did speak with Albert. He did not welcome what I had to say, but I was insistent to the point of disrespect. I'm glad he came to hear more."

"After you met with the king, His Majesty summoned me that afternoon. He asked me about how you helped me get my ring back. I told him what I know to be the truth but mentioned that du Pais and Albert had tried to convince me otherwise. I then confessed my indiscretion to him when I mentioned to Wim how you had helped me, Pierre and Sir John. Our interview ended shortly after."

"Since then, we have heard nothing," Lucy added. "There is a rumor that Wim left the castle late last night, after dark."

"Well, I thank you both for your help and support," I said humbly. "Without it, I would not be sitting here."

"Enough of all that," Freddy stated. "The Queen's Cup is tomorrow, and the entire city is in a jovial mood. I suggest we try to match it."

He rose and went to the door. He stuck his head out and spoke with someone outside. When he returned, he left the door open.

"Lunch will be served presently," he announced. "Lucy tells me you have some shopping to do this afternoon."

I chuckled. "She told me the same thing. She also informed me I am escorting her to the race and will be sitting in the family box."

"Nervous, Caz?" he asked.

I nodded.

"You should be," he said ominously.

"Stop it, Freddy!" Lucy snapped.

Freddy pretended to be aggrieved. "I'm just pointing out that there are certain protocols and procedures that one must follow before being permitted to court a woman of your standing, Lady Darling."

"Freddy, he's terrified as it is. Don't make it worse," she warned.

Fortunately, lunch arrived, interrupting us. While we ate, Freddy shared that Lucy's father, the Duke of Gulick, whom he referred to as 'Uncle Noel,' was almost completely lacking in pretension. "He will be much more interested in the race than in you," he stated.

"Who is the favorite?" I asked. "I haven't paid any attention, as you know. I'd like to have some idea before we arrive."

That led Freddy into a dissertation of the strengths and weaknesses of the three horses he felt were the favorites. Then he began to discuss their owners and then the jockeys. He finished with a discussion of recent weather. It had rained for two days while I was imprisoned, and Freddy felt that might slow the race, with the presumably soft turf giving an advantage to one and handicapping another.

When he finished, I asked, "So, who will you put your money on?"

"Well, I'll have to see how I feel tomorrow," he said. "And I'll have to take a look at the animals before the race. Then, after I—"

"If there is a good-looking grey horse in the field, Freddy will put his money on it," Lucy interrupted with a laugh. "As he always does. All your analysis and careful study goes flying away, Freddy, when you see a handsome grey."

Freddy shrugged his shoulders. "It's a weakness," he admitted.

After lunch, Lucy and I went to my tailor. When he saw us, he bustled into his back room. He came out with an armload of clothing. He took it behind a screen and instructed me to change so he could check the fit. I was perplexed, wondering when Lucy had instructed him to begin work. He could not have prepared all this in the few hours since I was released.

The dominant color was a shade of cream for the breeches, waistcoat and jacket. There were accents in blue and tan. I would have to compare, but the blue seemed close to the color of Lucy's eyes and the tan—more of a wheat color—a close match to her hair. The stockings, shirt and cravat were white.

When I put on the new clothes, everything fit well. This tailor had my measurements on file from earlier purchases. The fabric felt luxurious—more sumptuous than anything else I owned. I walked out in my stockinged feet and presented myself for inspection. The tailor fussed but eventually decided he did not need to make any alterations. When I looked in the mirror, I called Lucy over. Standing beside her, I could see the color of the accent stripes did indeed match her eyes and hair.

I changed back into the clothing I was wearing. The tailor swooped behind the screen and gathered the new clothes. He folded and arranged them in a neat bundle, which he wrapped in paper and tied with twine.

"How much do I owe you?" I asked.

The tailor gave me a pained expression. "Ordinarily, sur, I'd ask for forty ducats. Seeing as how I had to drop nearly everything to get this finished in three days, I'm afraid I must ask for fifty."

This was more than three times what I'd paid for any other suit of clothes I'd bought from the man. He knew it as well as I did. Knowing that Lucy had ordered this, I stifled my objection.

"I will come on Monday to settle my account with you," I informed him.

"Thank you, sur," he replied.

I put the bundle under my left arm and offered my right to Lucy. We exited the tailor's and I steered us to the cobbler. There would be no time for him to make me a new pair of boots. I would need to buy a pair he had already constructed that might not fit as well.

We entered his shop. He looked up from his bench. "There you are, Mr. FitzDuncan. Your timing is almost perfect. I'm just finishing the boots Lady Darling ordered for you."

I looked at Lucy and began to chuckle. She smirked at me in response. I shook my head.

A few more taps of his hammer and the cobbler finished. He brought a pair of boots of dark brown leather. He indicated I should sit and try them on to make sure they fit. Like the tailor, the cobbler had my measurements on file. He had carved wooden forms, called lasts, that mimicked the shape of my feet.

The leather was buttery soft. I pulled the boots on and they seemed to caress my calves. They fit my feet perfectly. I told him so.

"Then you won't complain when I charge you ten ducats for them," he said.

I raised my eyebrows in response. That was twice what I'd paid for any previous boots.

"It's a better grade of leather than you've chosen before, Mr. FitzDuncan," he explained. "Plus, Lady Darling gave me only three days to make them."

"It's not a problem, Simon," I replied.

I reached into my pocket and withdrew the handkerchief in which I had my money. After counting out ten ducats, I handed the coins to him. I asked if he could have his boy deliver them to my rooms, along with my bundle of new clothes. He agreed without hesitation.

Leaving his shop, we walked two doors down to the glover. He also made money pouches. I bought two, just in case. I transferred my remaining funds from the handkerchief into one of the new pouches and put the other pouch in my pocket.

When we left his shop, I halted out in the street. I clasped Lucy's gloved hands. "Lucy, we need to talk. Please don't deflect me the way you do."

We went to her rooms above her shop. She sat in a chair. I pulled the low stool over to sit near her. I clasped her hands.

From the moment I told her we needed to talk, sadness and worry had overtaken her. I didn't want to make her sad—quite the opposite. I did need to have her explain some things.

"Lucy, you had the tailor and cobbler begin work the day I met with the king," I stated. "You are one of the kindest hearts I've encountered, so I know you would not have them do the work without hope of payment. That means you knew, somehow, that the king would set me free. There are other things I've seen you do, like when you made Freddy remember his conversation with Wim. When I have tried to think about the things I've seen you do, I am unable to pursue those thoughts. I find myself distracted by pleasant thoughts of you. If I were to guess, I'm guessing that you are allowing me to question you right now. Please. Tell me as much as you think I can understand."

"When we met, I told you I could perceive your aura," she said. "Most people, including my family, think that I'm making that up. You believe me. Well, that's one of my abilities. I can prevent people from analyzing my abilities. You've noticed that."

"So has Freddy," I commented.

"Freddy has no idea I'm doing anything," she clarified. "He thinks I'm a witch and then he finds he no longer feels that way. That's how it works on most people."

"You seem to know where people are," I remarked.

"Only with certain people," she said. "And I have to know the location. I imagine them in a particular place and I know if I'm right."

"Another thing I've noticed is how touching you restores my self-confidence and optimism," I said.

"That's also true. I can do the opposite as well."

"How did you know the king would release me?" I asked. "Can you see the future?"

"Yes and no," she responded. "There are certain people whose auras are sympathetic to mine. If I touch them, I can see some of the parts of the future where we interact, back to what I call a 'hinge' moment. I call it a 'hinge' because it's where the future could change. Depending on what happens at the 'hinge' moment, the future I've seen will either come true or be completely different."

"This is one of those," I commented.

She nodded.

"Is that why you are sad and worried right now?"

She nodded.

"You saw that the king would release me and we would be together today?" I asked. "That's why you had the tailor and cobbler begin?"

"Yes," she whispered.

"What else can you do?" I asked.

"It's not time for me to share that," she said softly. "But I promise I will tell you when I can."

"One last question," I said. "I am just now remembering something from our first meeting. You mentioned that Freddy has no magical ability, and he asked why you singled out him and didn't include me. You didn't answer. Without jeopardizing our future, can you—"

Lucy leaped from the chair, threw her arms around my neck, and started kissing me all over my face. Her hat came askew but didn't fall off. Her lips found mine. Her mouth opened and her tongue invaded, looking for mine. Though I was as confused as I could be, I am also a warm-blooded male and responded in kind. When we separated to gasp for breath, I pushed her up so I could look into her eyes. Though full of tears, the sadness and worry were gone, replaced by immense joy.

"We just passed the hinge moment?" I asked.

She nodded, biting her lower lip.

"What now?"

"When Grand-Nan learned I had this ability, she warned me I cannot share my visions of the future with anyone. If I do, I create new hinge moments. I've since looked it up and learned she was correct, as far as everything talented people have written down."

"So, you're telling me you'll always have secrets you'll keep from me," I teased.

She smirked. "Yes. Get used to it." In a more serious tone, she continued, "There will be times when I can't give you answers and will put you off until 'later.' You need to understand why."

"I think I do. Is discussing my potential a topic for later?"

"Mostly. Your aura shows something. It will be up to you to discover it."

"Will I discover it?" I asked.

"I don't know," she replied. "There are more people than you would suspect walking around who have potential but don't know it and never figure it out."

"There's something else I need to discuss," I mentioned.

"I know," she replied, smirking again. "What Freddy told you about my family is accurate. My father manages his holdings for the good of his tenants, not to amass a fortune. They prosper and are happy, but money is always tight in our family."

"Still, the kingdom would be better off if more followed your father's example. Tomorrow, when I ask your father for permission to court you—he will grant it?"

She nodded, still looking down at me.

"Is there anything else I should know that I haven't asked you?"

"Clever," she commented. "Yes. You're taking me to dinner."

"I could have told you that," I said.

"At the River House," she continued. "Our reservation is at seven o'clock. Freddy is coming to pick us up. Tomorrow, you've rented a gig. It will arrive outside your rooms at ten o'clock and you will pick me up at half-past."

"Good to know," I replied. "I heard the four o'clock bells as we arrived. What will we do for the next two hours or so?"

She answered me by lowering her lips to mine.

# 12

We were both in a state of dishabille when we heard knocking on the door. "Lucy? The door is bolted," I heard Freddy call out.

We broke apart and scrambled to our feet. "Be right there," she called out. I shooed her into her bedroom to make herself presentable once again. I quickly straightened and tucked my clothes. There was a mirror near the door. I was glad I checked. My hair was mussed. I ran my fingers through it quickly. Freddy was standing on the landing, looking impatient. He examined me carefully.

"Greta is waiting in the carriage," he said gruffly. "Please get Lucy to hurry along."

He turned and trotted downstairs. Just as he left, Lucy emerged, rearranging her hair. She carried a light green shawl that complemented the color of her dress. I took the shawl. After waiting for her to tug on her gloves, I helped drape it over her shoulders.

"Who is Greta?" I asked as we went down the stairs.

"Ratty Hawkins' younger sister."

"I didn't know he had one."

"He does. She and Freddy are quite fond of one another. That is a good thing since the families are negotiating right now."

"Negotiating? About what?"

"About Freddy marrying Greta."

"My, my," I replied.

I held the carriage door for Lucy and handed her in. When she had tucked her skirts out of the way, I clambered in myself. Greta was sitting in the corner opposite to me.

"I apologize for our tardiness," I stated. "We lost track of the hour."

"Greta, may I present Casimir FitzDuncan," Freddy said, introducing us. "He's an old friend from school days. Caz, this is Greta Hawkins."

"A pleasure to meet you, miss," I stated. "I know your brother, I believe."

Greta is petite and, well, 'cute' is the word that springs to mind. Her head came to just above Lucy's shoulder. Her features are delicate, almost elfin. Her dark hair was done up in braids that began at her temples and gathered in a bun. Her dress was a dark blue that matched her eyes, in a similar style to Lucy's.

"A bastard and a merchant's daughter," she commented wryly. "Slumming it tonight, Freddy?"

I barked a laugh before I could help myself. Lucy smirked. Freddy relaxed his posture and lowered his eyelids halfway.

"Yas," he drawled in what I was calling his 'Lord Rawlinsford' voice. "Lady Darling and I feel duty-bound to spend time occasionally with the less fortunate, you see. One evening enduring the company of the likes of you two and we will have fulfilled our moral obligation until mid-winter, at least. Don't you agree, Lady Darling?"

Lucy drew herself up primly, moving on the seat as far away from Greta as the confines of the carriage would permit. She gave a haughty sniff as her response, as though actually speaking to us was too far beneath her. Again, I laughed involuntarily.

"Milord, milady, I apologize for presuming to join you in the carriage," I said humbly, knuckling my forelock. "If you'll ask the coachman to stop, I'll go ride with him."

Lucy again replied with a sniff.

"I'd say the evening is off to a wonderful start, wouldn't you, Miss Hawkins?" I remarked.

It was Greta's turn to have a laugh escape. She tried to choke it back, and it ended up coming out as a squeak. The strange sound made me laugh anew, with Freddy and Lucy joining in.

The rest of the evening was delightful. Greta has a wonderful sense of humor. It was three hours of sharing good food and better company. We laughed hard and often, drawing looks from other diners.

After dinner, we climbed back into the carriage. I made a half-hearted attempt to climb up with the coachman, but Lucy pulled me back. We reached my rooms first. I gave Lucy a brief kiss on the lips and waved goodbye.

What a satisfying feeling it was to be in my own bed after more than a week away! Before I drifted off the sleep, I remembered to thank all the gods for my deliverance. I also thanked them for my friends. The last was a prayer to Freyja, the goddess of romance, asking her blessings on whatever was developing between Lucy and me.

I woke in a light-hearted mood, though later than my normal custom. After washing up, I put on yesterday's clothes and went in search of breakfast. I went to the Foaming Boar since I needed to settle my account with Carl

Stensland. He was pleased to see me. I thanked him for his assistance and told him the matter had been resolved successfully. He gave me a bill that seemed too low. I tried to argue with him, but he waved me off.

As I was climbing the stairs to my rooms, I heard the bells for ten o'clock. I changed into my new finery. I put extra funds in my money pouch so Lucy and I could bet on the races. After that, I did not wait long. I saw the gig arrive from my window and hurried down. The boy who delivered it told me he would return at ten that evening. If the gig were not there, he would return at ten the next morning, but the livery would charge extra. I gave him two demi-florins for his trouble.

It was a clear, bright fall day. The temperature, chilly earlier, was warming as the sun rose higher. There were no clouds. I climbed into the gig. Retrieving the reins, I gave them a flick and we set off to Lucy's. The horse was well-trained and amiable. She would never win a race but was well-suited for a pleasant journey to the Queen's Cup.

Arriving at Lucy's, I went to the outside entrance at the rear. I climbed the stairs and knocked on the door. Her beauty made me gasp. Where to begin? Like Greta last night, her hair was braided, starting at her temples. It swept behind her head until it formed an elegant knot at the nape of her neck. Her dress was a light grey, with flowers embroidered on the bodice. The petals of the flowers were the same color blue and wheat as the accents on my breeches, waistcoat and jacket, matching the color of her eyes and hair. She carried a broad-brimmed straw hat. She told me she would put it on when we arrived at the race. She put on gloves of grey kid that matched her dress.

I escorted her to the gig and helped her in. After circling to my side, I climbed in. "Lucy, you are a vision," I said sincerely. "I must ask. When we met, and for days after, you wore loose, comfortable dresses and let your hair fly free. Yesterday and today, you are the picture of elegance."

"Both are real, Caz," she responded before I could finish. "The little girl who lives across the alley helped me with my hair today. When we finished, she said, 'Why, Miss Lucy. You're a *Lady*.' I told her yes but I was also still just Miss Lucy. I dress for comfort most of the time, but I am no stranger to fine clothes. I enjoy dressing up more than I did as a girl because I only do it when I want to, not when Mother demands."

"I think I understand," I said. "One thing is certain. I will be the envy of every man there today."

We rode to the course. Only one race was held on the course every year— the Queen's Cup. The course was just under a league and a half long. The course was a long oval with two long, straight sections. It started at the left-hand side of the straight nearest the grandstands and finished on the right-hand side, meaning horses traveled the front straight twice. There were thirty jumps the horses and riders must clear from start to finish. Some were fences or hedges, requiring the horse to jump high. Others were ditches, requiring the horse to jump for distance. Four were fences with ditches behind. The front straight held a hedge, a ditch, a high fence and a low fence with a ditch behind. From the grandstands, one could see the entire race. The start and the finish took place immediately in front of the stands.

The entire event had a festival atmosphere. Even commoners, those who could afford the entrance fee, dressed in their finest to attend the race. Most of the seating in the grandstand was egalitarian, except for family boxes. Fanning out behind the Royal Box, the family boxes were cordoned off groups of seats, controlled by different noble families. The number of family boxes is half what it used to be. To maintain a claim on a family box, the head of the family must make a sizeable donation to a charity of the queen's choice. Should a family fail to meet its obligation, they lose the box.

My grandfather had maintained a box, but my father let it lapse. If he wished to attend the race, he might find himself sitting next to a common tradesman. Most embraced the spirit of the event, where the usual barriers between the classes were ignored. A few years after this, Linc Ellsworth, whose family gave up their box, declared to us he had never enjoyed a race more or eaten better than when he sat with a smith's family who came all the way from Corneva.

The race was the last of the season and the longest. The course tested the skill and stamina of both horse and rider. It was rare that one horse would win by a substantial margin. Generally, there was a group of three-to-five entering the last straight that had a chance to win. It was exciting to be part of a crowd of nearly a hundred thousand, all yelling for his or her favorite to win.

As I mentioned before, the race was only part of the event. It was a social occasion. Strolling the grounds, watching people dressed in their finest— that was part of the entertainment as well.

We rode to the entrance of the grounds. I helped Lucy from the gig. Then I drove to where all the various carriages, carts, wagons and other conveyances were to stay during the race. I fastened the horse's lead to a post and hurried back to find Lucy. Thankfully, she was with Freddy and Greta. Otherwise, I suspected a group of eager young men would have surrounded her.

"How did you get back so quickly?" I asked Freddy.

He grinned evilly. "Theo drove us."

Lucy and I began to laugh. Greta looked puzzled. Freddy explained about the frosty relationship I had with Theo.

Freddy was eager to walk to the paddock to examine the horses. We ambled over as a group, taking in the sights. I caught several men casting jealous glances my way. It made me want to preen like a peacock. When we reached the paddock, Freddy pointed out the three horses he had discussed

117

in his lengthy dissertation at lunch the day before. When I saw a handsome grey horse, I brought it to Lucy's attention.

"Freddy, what about number nine over there?" Lucy asked, referring to the grey.

"Oh!" Freddy sighed. "What a beauty!" He looked over to the side to check the tote board. "Too bad he doesn't have a hope of winning."

The board showed the odds on nine as being 150-1. "What does that mean?" Greta asked.

I explained, "If you bet on number nine to win the race, and he does, the bookmakers who handle the betting will pay you 150 times what you bet."

"The number four horse is listed as 3-2," she said. "What does that mean?"

"If you bet, say, two florins, and the horse won, they would pay you three florins and also return the two you bet. You would have five florins from risking two."

"Does that mean the number four horse is better than the number nine?" she inquired.

"The numbers change based on the amount of the bets placed. It means that lots of people are betting, risking their money, thinking the number four horse will win," I explained. "Not many think the number nine will win."

After Freddy was satisfied he'd seen what he wanted to see, we strolled back toward the grandstand. When we reached the booths of the bookmakers, I pulled Lucy aside. I opened my money pouch.

"Lucy, here's twenty ducats to make some bets," I said. "Place your bets however you wish, but don't tell me what you did until after the race starts. I'm going to do the same."

"Caz, I have my own money," she protested.

"I know. It just gives me pleasure to let you play with mine. Oh—what you win, you keep," I clarified.

I left Lucy looking at the tote board. I walked into the booth and waited until I reached the front of the line. The tote board had changed slightly since we saw it at the paddock. The grey horse was now listed at 180-1.

Until recently in my life, I could not explain why I did what I did. At the time, I might have blamed my sense of humor or claimed it was out of loyalty to Freddy or told you I had a hunch. I put twenty ducats on the grey. The bookmaker didn't react, just wrote out my bet on the stub of paper, stamped it and handed it back. I went back outside and waited for Lucy.

She handed me her stub. I put it with mine in my pouch without looking at it. She tucked her left hand in my elbow.

"I'm hungry," she said.

Is there anything better than the simple food at such events? Cooked meat on a stick, dough fried in bubbling oil and sprinkled with sugar or honey? Many call such things peasant food and look down their noses at it.

Me? I call it delicious and thoroughly enjoy the one or two times each year that I can indulge.

Fortunately, Lucy felt the same. The sight of her, in her beautiful dress, gnawing at some meat on a stick, leaning forward so no grease would drip on her—I treasure that memory. Sharing a piece of light dough sprinkled with sugar, as wide as a dinner plate, is another. We licked our fingers clean when we finished, sharing a naughty grin like schoolchildren.

When our tongues had cleaned our fingers as well as they could, I offered her my handkerchief. She wiped her fingers. Then I did the same. She put her gloves back on and clasped my arm again. We heard the first bell warning that the race would start soon.

"Time to face your reckoning, I think," she said.

We entered the grandstand area. She knew exactly where to go and guided me. We climbed the stairs past the Royal Box. I saw the king and queen in attendance, along with Albert. Unlike past years, Albert had none of his friends with him.

When we were halfway between the Royal Box and the top row, she tugged me gently to the right. It occurs to me you may have a more grand impression of what these boxes were. The Royal Box, it is true, was separated by low wooden partitions and contained proper furniture on which to sit. A family box was nothing like that. It was merely a section marked off by twine tied between posts. The seats were planks, like the rest of the grandstand. The only advantage would be extra room if only a few guests were invited. Since friends and more distant relatives would plead for the opportunity to sit in a box, conditions were usually just as crowded as everywhere else.

There were a half-dozen people in the area denoted as her family's box. I lifted the twine so Lucy could go under without removing her hat, then ducked under myself. She took me to a tall man. The set of his eyes was identical to Lucy's.

"Father, I would like to introduce Casimir FitzDuncan. Caz, my father."

I bowed, saying, "Your Grace."

When I straightened, I noticed a hint of Lucy's smirk on his face. He responded by offering me his hand. That was a pleasant surprise.

As we shook hands, he said, "I've heard a little about you from my cousin, Freddy's father. He thinks well of you."

"Thank you, Your Grace," I replied.

"What are your intentions toward my daughter?" His tone changed from polite to intimidating. He had not released my hand and was, in fact, gripping it firmly as though to trap me. He looked into my eyes without blinking.

Though his change in demeanor rattled me, I stood my ground. I continued to look him right in the eyes and answered, "Your Grace, I would like permission to court your daughter, Lucy."

He maintained his glare for a moment, then broke into a wide smile, releasing my hand as he did. "You may," he said.

"Thank you, Your Grace."

"Casimir, my name is Noel. I'd prefer if you use that instead."

"My friends call me, 'Caz.'"

"Caz, you're the first young man Lucy has shown any interest in. I hope we don't scare you away," he said.

"Daddy!" Lucy complained.

The second set of bells rang, warning the race was about to start. Looking down at the course, I could see the horses and riders making their way to the starting line. The three favorites, numbers four, six and seven, seemed spirited and eager. They were tossing their heads, with nostrils slightly flared, excited to begin the race. The grey on which I'd bet seemed completely disinterested, plodding alongside the course with his head down.

The horses all reached the starting line. The final set of warning bells rang. Officials arranged the horses in the correct order. An official dropped a flag and the race began.

Lucy gripped my hand as the horses surged forward. After clearing the second obstacle, a ditch, as they neared us, the three favorites pulled ahead of the rest. My grey was toward the rear of the group of the other six. The third obstacle was a high fence.

The grey jumped far too high and when he landed, his rider almost pitched to the ground over the horse's neck. The next was the low fence with the ditch behind. The grey's jump was lazy. His back hooves splashed the water, and he stumbled slightly as a result. He was now in last place. When horse and rider recovered from the stumble, they trailed by five lengths. A dozen lengths separated the grey from the three favorites.

I was shaking my head, regretting my whimsy at putting my money on him. There was a reason he had such long odds. As I was thinking this, the grey seemed to realize he was in a race after all. He pinned his ears back and lunged his head forward. He began to pick up ground. After three more obstacles, he had caught up to the pack. By the time he was on the far side of the course, opposite from where we were, he had nosed to just in front of the pack. The last of the three favorites was still four lengths ahead, though.

Lucy's hand, which had relaxed its grip on my hand when the grey was floundering, tightened. Leaving the back straight and coming around the curve, the grey continued to gain ground. Entering the final straight, the grey's nose was even with the saddle of the third horse. The crowd was on its feet, yelling and shouting.

"Come on, Trooper!" Lucy screamed.

"Trooper?" I asked.

"The grey," she responded.

"Come on, Trooper!" I bellowed.

There were four obstacles left. The first was a hedge. When they touched the ground, Trooper was now in third place by a hand span. The riders of the three favorites were smacking their mounts with their crops, trying to urge them to greater speed. Trooper's rider never touched his crop. His hands were on the reins as he leaned forward. It almost looked as though he were talking to the grey.

Approaching the next obstacle, a ditch, Trooper had caught the second horse. His jump was perfectly timed and he landed in stride, even with the second horse. The spectators were screaming and hollering. The noise was deafening. Lucy and I added to it, urging Trooper on.

The next obstacle was the high fence. Trooper had jumped too high and almost thrown his rider the first time. His nose was even with the lead horse's shoulder when they reached it. This jump was perfect—his belly must have rubbed the top rail. On the way to the last obstacle, the low fence and ditch where he stumbled, Trooper seemed to gain inches with every stride. The two horses left the ground at the same moment, leaping over the final obstacle.

From our angle, we could not see which was ahead. When the two crossed the finish line, there was an even louder roar from that section of the stands. Then the cheering began. Whether your pick won or lost, we had just witnessed a marvelous race.

Lucy turned to me and buried her head in my shoulder. "I can't look," she said.

She was referring to the pole at the officials' station at the finish. The officials would attach flags showing the finishing order. In a moment, they hauled the flags up briskly. When the breeze snapped them open, many in the crowd groaned. I didn't.

"Trooper won," I whispered to Lucy.

She raised her head and turned to see for herself. She began to laugh her merry, joyous laugh. She threw her arms around my neck and began kissing me rapidly, again and again. When she stopped kissing me, she began laughing again.

The crowd was beginning to leave. Her father stopped at us. "Don't tell me you bet on the grey," he said.

Lucy released her grip around my neck and turned to him. "Fine, Daddy. I won't tell you."

"Both of you?" he asked.

I nodded. "Majors and Minors," he muttered. He began chuckling as he walked down the steps.

We went to the bookmakers' booths. There certainly wasn't a crowd. Not many had bet on Trooper. I approached the counter and showed our betting slips to the man.

"You and the missus are going to be among the few who leave here happy today," he commented.

He examined our slips. "Final odds were 200-1. I can pay you here or I can write you a bank draft."

"Bank draft, please," I requested.

"Name?"

"We'll need two," I said.

"Oh? I thought you was married."

"Not yet," Lucy quipped. "Maybe this will help."

"Fine. First one?" he asked.

Lucy looked at me, making an attempt to give me the money. I shook my head. "Lucille…" I began.

"Lucille Austermain," she said and spelled her last name.

"And you?" he asked.

"Casimir FitzDuncan." I spelled my first name.

He finished writing, then handed me the bank drafts. I folded them and tucked them in my pouch. Bank drafts were much more sensible than trying to lug a large enough chest to contain 8,000 ducats.

We left and went to the entrance. There was still a crowd of people waiting for carriages. We saw Freddy and Greta and walked over to them. Freddy looked glum. When he saw us, he shook his finger at Lucy.

"It's all your fault," he said.

"What's my fault?"

"After you teased me at dinner last night, I didn't dare bet on the grey, especially with such ridiculous odds. Did you know he went off at 200-1? Majors and Minors! The one time in my life I *should* have bet on the grey, I didn't! I blame you. Arrgh!" he shouted.

Lucy and I tried to keep our faces neutral. Lucy broke first and began laughing. That set me off. In moments, we were holding onto one another to keep from falling since we were laughing so hard. Greta started laughing just because we were.

Freddy glared at me. "What?" he demanded. "Why is this so funny?"

That, of course, made us laugh harder. It took some time for us to calm down. Lucy had her hand on my shoulder as she bent over slightly, trying to catch her breath.

"Freddy, dear," she said between gasps. "We both bet on the grey."

That started me laughing again, and Lucy joined me. Greta, now aware of what the cause of our laughter was, began to produce deep guffaws. Such a deep sound coming from her petite frame was so incongruous that Freddy began to laugh.

When we recovered, I asked Freddy and Greta if they would keep Lucy company while I fetched the gig. They agreed. On my way out to the field, I saw Theo sitting with the coachman on the open carriage that Freddy had hired for the day. I waved to him cordially. He stared at me in response.

I retrieved the gig without difficulty and rode back to the entrance.

Freddy waved me off and helped his cousin into her seat. He then helped Greta into the carriage, and they set off with a wave.

"Drive slow," Lucy asked.

"I don't think she has any other gait than slow," I replied.

Lucy took off her hat, unpinning it from her hair. She then slid over the seat to me. She clutched my arm, kissed my cheek, then leaned her head on my shoulder. "This has been a marvelous day," she commented.

I put my arm around her shoulders and bent to kiss the top of her head. "Yes, it has," I agreed.

# 13

When I returned to my rooms that evening, I left the gig tied out front, as the boy instructed. I took off my fine clothes and put on something far less fancy, though I did put the new boots back on. They were the most comfortable pair I'd worn. It occurred to me that if my relationship with Lucy continued, she might insist on improving my wardrobe. Though she dressed for comfort and practicality most of the time, I wondered if I would be allowed the same consideration. I doubted it.

That evening I visited another inn, the Green Knight. The dinner was passable, but the atmosphere was fun. There was a rowdy crowd that had come straight from the race and been drinking ever since. They were all well past the point of being tipsy but were a merry group of drunks. All of them had lost money at the race but didn't care. The general agreement was that it had been the best race in many years.

After dinner, I returned to my rooms. I kicked off my boots and settled down with a book. One tremendous advantage to owning a bookseller is always having something interesting to read.

In the morning, I went to the Temple of the Three Major Gods near my rooms. I had many reasons to thank the Gods. I offered a pinch of incense to all the Majors, then went outside to the shrines of the Minors and did the same. Afterward, I returned to my rooms. It began to rain. Though I considered going to visit Lucy, I did not want her to tire of my company. I spent the day reading, staying dry and warm.

The next day, I set out early. After getting a spot of breakfast, I settled accounts with the livery and my tailor. I complimented him on the fine job he'd done. Following that, I headed to Pierre Luin's office.

After meeting Pierre and helping him with his indiscretion, I learned more about what he did. In simple terms, he managed money for people who had a lot of it. About four years ago, he helped me negotiate the purchase of the bookseller from Lyle Forteney. As a result, he learned how much cash I was sitting on.

He sat me down and explained how I could use my money to earn money. He offered to take me on as a client. Even though I would be his smallest, he was still grateful for my help a couple of years earlier. Through Pierre, I became a part-owner of several buildings and businesses in the city. Owning a share of a building, along with a number of other investors, spread the risk between us. The income from the rents was also split, but it meant that my money was earning more money.

I was stopping by to hand over the bank draft from the bookmaker. 4,020 ducats was a good amount, and I was sure Pierre would find something to buy that would generate more income. When I entered his office, he brought me in.

"How did things work out on that affair you mentioned to me?" he asked.

"Satisfactorily," I replied.

I handed over the bank draft. He was, no doubt, expecting it to be related to what we had discussed. When he saw it was from the bookmaker, his eyes grew wide.

"You bet on the grey?" he asked, incredulous.

I smiled and nodded.

"I wish I'd had the balls," he commented. "Great race, though. A great day all around."

He asked if I had any specific idea what I wanted to do with the money. I shook my head. He wrote out a receipt for 4,020 ducats and gave it to me.

"If you continue to add to your investments for another few years at the same rate you have been, you might be able to retire. I'd say, in six or seven years."

"What if I get married?" I asked. I don't know why I asked that. It seemed to jump out of me.

Pierre raised his eyebrows. "I thought you were a committed bachelor, Caz. Someone has caught your fancy, eh?"

"I don't know why I even said that, Pierre. I've only known the woman for about a fortnight," I explained.

"I don't mean to tease you, Caz. I hope it works out," Pierre said. "To answer your question, marrying might delay your retirement. Having children definitely will. Children are expensive."

"Did that stop you?" I asked, knowing Pierre had three children.

He laughed. "Heavens no! Is there anything else I can help you with?"

We reviewed my accounts. I thought I had done well for myself (and had, with all due modesty). I asked Pierre what opportunities we were overlooking.

"Cargo," he replied. "You can buy a portion of a ship's cargo from one of the big merchants. When the ship arrives, and the cargo sells, you get a portion of the profits. Investments of this type pay three times more than your current holdings."

"Why aren't we doing that?" I asked.

"The minimum cost is ten thousand ducats," Pierre explained. "The risk is also greater. Wind and weather don't discriminate. I would be uncomfortable putting such a large portion of your funds in a single investment that could sink. In the future, with continued success on both our parts, we will talk about this again."

After taking my leave of Pierre, it was just past ten o'clock. My thigh was aching, so I hailed a hackney to return to my rooms. When I paid the cabbie, I turned around. Forteney was there. He held a piece of paper in his hand.

"A boy delivered this for you about an hour ago," he said.

The paper was unsealed. I unfolded it.

> If you want to see Lady Darling alive, you must come to the du Pais estate immediately. Come alone. If you are accompanied, she dies. Come quickly. If you arrive after nightfall or do not come, she will suffer unspeakable consequences, then she will die. Please hurry. Your Ladylove and I await. Wim

All my earlier good feeling was forgotten. The crumpled letter in my hand, I began to run toward the Foaming Boar as fast as I could, though my thigh slowed me. I burst through the front and immediately began yelling for Carl. He came out from the kitchen, wiping his hands.

"Sar'nt, I need to borrow your horse."

He could see I was in a panic. "Sure," he said. "You know where he is."

I called my thanks over my shoulder as I darted past him, through the kitchen and out the back. Andy was in his stall. I found his tack. Forcing myself to slow down so I wouldn't forget anything, I saddled him as quickly as I could.

As quickly as we could travel through the crowded streets, we made our way to the North Gate. Though the temptation is to gallop away, I knew enough from my stint in the Rangers not to. If I did, the horse would be exhausted long before we reached the destination. So, despite my sense of urgency, I set Andy to trot. We would alternate trotting and walking. Frustrating though it was to move more slowly, we would make it before nightfall as long as nothing happened to delay us.

When we passed the swale where we had tried to intercept Miss Traval, I realized I no longer was clutching the letter in my hand. I wondered where I dropped it. It wasn't important, I decided.

Weather moved in as we traveled. By the time we were a league outside the city, rain clouds hung over the road in front of us. When the rain hit, I slowed Andy to a walk. The rain was cold, and I was drenched quickly. I kept Andy at a walk until I judged we had covered half a league, then bumped him back to a trot.

Wim had taken Lucy to draw me out of the city alone. He wanted revenge, I reckoned, since I had ruined his plot. I reviewed in my mind what happened in the shrine. This was hardly the first time I had revisited those moments; it must have been hundreds of times by then. I reached the same conclusion I had before.

Wim must not have seen me knock Albert out. He thought I'd killed him. By the time he discovered Albert was merely unconscious, his men were in the room, or Wim would have killed him. Wim couldn't see because the door opened the wrong way. Something as trivial as which way a door opened had made all the difference. Whether I killed Bergeron or Bergeron killed me was unimportant—the survivor would get the blame. Whether Albert lived or died was different. Albert surviving was a complication. Albert surviving, and deciding to listen to what I had to say, was a disaster.

Wim wanted to kill me or wanted me to kill him. Would Wim harm Lucy? The Wim I thought I knew would never have done such a thing. The Wim who concocted the obscene plot that just unraveled—I didn't know him. He might do unspeakable things to her.

We reached a village. I made sure Andy got some water. We kept going after he drank. I tried to spend an equal amount of time with Andy walking and trotting. The rain continued.

My stomach was letting me know I missed lunch and the dinner hour was nearing. The rain stopped. I judged we had traveled just short of eight leagues when we reached another village. I allowed Andy to drink, then tied him to the post in front of the inn. I entered and asked for two things. One was some bread. I waited until it was in my hand to ask the second question. I needed to find the du Pais estate. As I guessed, that request was not received as well.

"Why do you want to know?" asked the man behind the bar as the patrons glared at me.

"A madman kidnapped the woman I love and told me to meet him there before nightfall," I blurted out, not thinking.

The man looked at me strangely. He must have thought I was joking. When I didn't follow up with a witty remark, understanding dawned upon him.

"Right. Keep heading away from the city. You won't go half a league until you see an overgrown allée of yew trees on the right. It's so overgrown you won't think it leads anywhere. Follow that to the main house. Good luck, friend."

"How much for the bread?" I asked.

He shook his head. I nodded my thanks, went out, and climbed back up on Andy. We left the village. The sky was clearing, but the temperature dropped. My clothes were soaked, and I felt the cold seeping into my bones.

Andy and I reached the allée. If the weeds had not been knocked down by the passage of the du Pais carriage recently, they would have been waist-high. Though I wanted to gallop to the rescue, I kept Andy at a walk. I did not want to risk injury on such uncertain ground.

We exited the allée. I could see the house. As Freddy had told me over a week before, it was in poor condition. The lawn and garden were badly overgrown. We rode to the front entrance. I dismounted and drew my sword.

"Ho! The house!" I bellowed.

The front door opened slowly. Wim stood there. He grinned.

"Where is Lucy?" I demanded.

"Inside."

"I want to see her."

"Come inside," he said politely, with a bow and a sweep of his arm.

"No. Bring her to the door."

"Why?

"So I know whether to kill you quickly or slowly," I answered, trying to project as much menace into my voice as I could.

He disappeared inside. I could hear scuffling noises and grunts. He dragged a chair outside. He'd tied Lucy to the arms and legs. A scarf was tied over her mouth, gagging her. Lucy was squirming and trying to yell. She was wearing the loose, comfortable type of dress she wore in the shop. Her hair was wild and free.

I looked at her, trying to show her how much I cared for her and how confident I was. And I was confident, surprisingly so. Wim was far better with a blade than his brother. It didn't matter to me. He might be a good fencer, but I would bite, kick, gouge, and do anything I could to defeat him. He had taken my love. I didn't care about rules—I would not lose.

I shrugged my wet jacket off and wrapped it around my left forearm. He did the same. I beckoned him down the steps. He drew his sword and skipped down them, almost happily.

I strolled over to him as though to offer the traditional salute. When I reached the accustomed distance, I sprang at him and launched a furious attack. I had a strange awareness that I was fighting on a different level than ever before. Somehow I knew I was stronger, faster, more skilled than I'd ever been. Was it because I was fighting for Lucy? Or was it something else? He gave ground and barely managed to fend me off. His expression had changed. His confidence was gone, and I could see fear in his eyes.

I stopped my charge, wanting to gather myself for the next one. He was panting. I was breathing heavily. He thrust at me. I allowed his blade to penetrate the jacket wrapped around my arm. He might have grazed my skin underneath, but I didn't feel it. I swung my arm to further entangle his sword.

I stepped forward and punched him in the mouth with my hand wrapped in the swept hilt of my sword. On the backswing, I slashed at his throat.

He fell to dodge my slash and managed to pull his sword free. I kicked him, catching his ribs as he tried to roll away. I allowed him to stagger to his feet. I could tell his side hurt from my kick. His face was a mess, with the pattern of my hilt embossed in his skin in bloody stripes.

"For a long time, I thought you were a better man than your brother, Wim," I said. "I was wrong."

"You're just a bastard," he sneered. "What would you know?"

"I know I'm not going to die today," I said.

I launched another furious attack. His third parry was too slow, and I sliced the front of his right thigh. Two strikes after that, his parry was weak, and I muscled through it and the tip of my blade penetrated his waistcoat and shirt, drawing a diagonal red line across his chest.

"I'll give you a gentleman's choice, Wim," I stated. "You can fall to your knees right now, and I promise I'll kill you quickly. Or I will play with you the way a cat plays with a trapped mouse."

He didn't like the choices I gave him. He tried to attack. I had never been faster. My vision had never been keener. I could see what he was going to do before his muscles started to move. He was tired, he was hurt—I stepped inside his clumsy attack after his third blow and buried my blade up under his ribs. I hit heart and lungs in one thrust. He knew he was dead when I pushed him away. An astonished look was on his face as he fell backward.

I wiped my blade using his jacket, then trotted up to Lucy. I untied the scarf from her head and quickly freed her wrists and ankles. She jumped into my arms, almost knocking me down the steps. Her arms around my neck, she buried her face in my chest. She wept with great wracking sobs.

I rubbed her back and stroked her hair, tucking her head under my chin. She continued to sob, so I began to murmur meaningless soft sounds, as one does to quiet a crying baby or calm a frightened animal. Eventually, the sobs subsided into crying. Her body stopped shaking.

With a sniff, she lifted her head and looked up at me. She was a mess. Her eyes were puffy and red-rimmed. Snot was dripping from her nose. She opened her mouth to say something and hiccupped instead. She started to laugh and cry at the same time. I reached into my pocket and withdrew my handkerchief.

"It's wet, but it's clean," I told her.

She wiped her eyes and blew her nose. She looked at my chest and wiped off some snot that collected there. She folded up the handkerchief and stuffed it in my pocket.

I noticed it had grown quite chilly. Her dress was thin. I straightened out my left arm and unwound my jacket from it. I draped it over her shoulders.

As I did, I noticed three large gashes in the fabric. My shirtsleeve was also cut and there was a thin line of drying blood on my forearm. It wasn't much more than a nasty scratch.

"It's wet," she said.

"I'm sorry. I hope it helps keep you warm. I'm wet all over. Andy and I came through a rainstorm."

"I know. Thank you."

"Shall we go?" I asked.

"Please. I don't like this place."

"Is there anyone inside?"

"No. There's no one here."

"There's an inn not far away. I'll get us rooms," I said.

She leaned back and moved her hands to my face. "Caz, one room, please. I don't want to be alone tonight."

I nodded. We walked to Andy. He was standing patiently. I wondered briefly what he might have thought about what he'd just seen. I helped Lucy up and climbed up behind her.

We rode down the weed-choked allée and out into the road. Daylight was fading. Halfway back to town, we encountered three riders heading our way. As they drew closer, I recognized Hank, Robby and Carl Stensland. I drew Andy to a stop.

"What brings you out this way, Sar'nt?" I asked.

"You did," Carl responded. "You left the note in the stable."

"Well, we're all done here," I said, avoiding specifics, hoping Carl had done the same. "Let's go back to the inn. I'll get us all rooms since it's too far to make it back to the city tonight."

"Robby, Hank, you two ride back to the inn," Carl instructed. "Mr. FitzDuncan and I are going to swap mounts. We'll be along shortly."

I dismounted and helped Lucy down. Carl got off the horse he was riding. We waited until the other two were out of earshot.

"I didn't tell them who wrote the note," Carl said.

"Good," I responded. "Lucy, tomorrow, would you mind riding back to the city with Hank and Robby? Carl and I need to take care of the body."

"Why?" she asked.

"I'll tell you later."

"Whose horse is he?" I asked Carl as I helped Lucy into the saddle.

"My brother-in-law's," Carl answered. "He's a good horse, but he's not Andy."

I swung up, and we rode back to the inn. They had three rooms left. Carl got one, Robby and Hank another, and Lucy and I the last. The innkeeper agreed to feed us. We retired to the rooms after dinner.

Lucy sat on the bed and I on the small chair in the room. "What are you going to do with the body?" she asked.

"Handle it discreetly," I said. "You told me that there was a rumor that Wim had left, but there was no 'official' news. If we can return the body to the castle discreetly, then they can decide how to announce his death. It will probably not include a kidnapping or the location being at the estate of a disgraced noble."

"I understand," she said, nodding.

"Now, as far as our sleeping arrangements, I will sleep on the floor," I announced.

"No."

"Lucy, I just received permission from your father to court you. That permission did not include anything more."

"It's not up to my father," Lucy said defiantly. She stood and crossed to me.

"It is up to me," she said. "If you insist on sleeping on the floor, then I will join you there. I think the bed would be more comfortable."

She sat on my lap. I tried to protest, but she silenced me with her lips. Our kissing grew more passionate. Lucy took my hands and placed them on her body where she desired. The fourth time we paused to catch our breath, she stood. She grasped her dress at the waist and lifted it over her head. She had only a thin shift on underneath. She took my hand and pulled me gently to bed.

Though I'm sure, dear readers, you are eager to know what happened next; I'm afraid I will have to disappoint you. A gentleman does not talk of such things. I may be a bastard, but I was raised a gentleman. More importantly, my love of Lucy is immeasurable. I hope never to tarnish it. I will tell you it was wonderful, tender, passionate and joyful.

When we woke, we made ourselves presentable. We joined the others downstairs and had some breakfast. Carl and I saw Lucy ride off with Hank and Robby. I then asked the innkeeper if I could buy two sheets from him. From what I'd mentioned the day before, he understood why I wanted them. I also had him give me a couple of loaves of bread since we didn't plan to stop that day. He added them to the bill, which I paid.

Carl and I returned to the du Pais estate. The body was where it fell. We brushed the flies away and rolled it in the sheets. Carl had some rope we used to tie the bundle to keep everything wrapped securely. We hoisted it up in front of the saddle of my horse and began the journey back to the city.

I judged it was about three o'clock when we reached the swale near the North Gate. Carl rode ahead while I turned off and pulled myself out of sight. I pulled Wim's dead body off the horse and let it thump onto the ground. There was a sapling nearby, so I took the horse and wrapped his reins around it, leaving him enough slack to graze if he wished.

I sat and waited. So many emotions were running through me. It was nice to be alone, even with a dead body for company.

Lucy had certainly escalated our relationship. I had lived my life alone to this point but was only occasionally lonely. That had changed dramatically and quickly. I now craved Lucy's company. I was on my guard, fearing that it was just infatuation (I'd never experienced it myself but had seen others afflicted and heard of the negative consequences).

I had killed a member of the royal family. Justified or not, it disturbed me on a deep level. Though the king had released me, I didn't think he was entirely pleased to do so. This would not improve his disposition toward me.

In the past two weeks, my emotions bounced up and down, occasionally to extremes. It made me uncomfortable. I was used to moderation.

Some of the things Lucy shared with me disquieted me. I had never believed in magic, though I had always feared it. She allowed me to see that it existed. I realized that was an act of intimacy and trust beyond even what we shared the night before. She told me I had latent ability but would not, or could not, tell me more. It was up to me to discover what it was.

If it were the ability to pick the winner of horse races, that was not so bad. Somehow I doubted the Major and Minor Gods would want magical talent used that way. I wondered if the feelings of strength and power I experienced in my fight with Wim were a sign. That would be an immense advantage, though in circumstances I hoped to encounter only rarely, if ever again.

Darkness arrived while I pondered. I had heard only a few travelers pass after dusk. The three-note whistle of a rail came from the road. It was a signal we used in the Rangers. I gave the same whistle in response. The whistle came from the road again.

Leaving the horse and body behind, I walked out to the road. Carl was there. By the light of the crescent moon, I could see a two-horse wagon on the road. Carl and I walked back and lifted the body. We carried it to the wagon and rolled it in over the side.

Returning to retrieve the horse, I recognized the driver of the wagon. "Your Highness," I said to Albert.

"FitzDuncan," he replied. To the best of my recollection, it is the first time he had ever addressed me directly by name.

"Please stop by tomorrow afternoon," he requested.

Albert flicked the reins and turned the horses back toward the city. I went back and unwrapped the reins. After leading him back to the road, I mounted. Carl and I rode back in silence.

# ABOUT THE AUTHOR

John Spearman (Jake to his friends and colleagues) is a Latin teacher and coach at a prestigious New England boarding school. Before joining the world of academia, Spearman had been a sales and marketing executive for 25 years. In 2006, he walked away from an executive position with a Fortune 500 company to return to school. He earned his M.A. in Latin in a calendar year and began teaching thereafter.

He began writing as a hobby. His first four books, the *Halberd* series, have been well-received, as has the first book of his *Pike* series. This book is foray into a new genre, unrelated to the earlier books.